"May I?" she asked.

He looked at her doubtfully. "I don't think so. Everybody from the maid to the elevator operator has tried to—"

Libby lifted the baby from his arms, smug with her insider knowledge that this particular infant was colicky and had responded well in the hospital to the football hold. The baby's sobs quietcd almost immcdiatcly.

The man was astounded. She smiled modestly.

"I was looking for Jared Ransom," she said, trying to look past him into the room to get a glimpse of the old fogy she'd come to see. But the man's broad shoulders filled the doorway.

His eyes moved from the baby to her face, roved it with a thoroughness that made her wonder what he could possibly be thinking.

Finally he said, "I'm Jared Ransom."

Libby clenched her teeth to prevent her jaw from dropping. The old fogy was gorgeous!

Dear Reader,

Have you ever wished you had a second chance at a once-in-a-lifetime opportunity? A chance to make another decision, to take a different path?

No doubt we all have. And that's why American Romance introduces you to four women who actually get that unique opportunity—whether it's to marry the one that got away or to have children or to follow an exciting career—in MAYBE THIS TIME.

Muriel Jensen brings this original quartet to a close with the story of a special woman destined to know the meaning of motherhood. It's another wonderful family story from this award-winning author.

Don't miss any of the MAYBE THIS TIME books—for stories that will touch a spot in every woman's heart!

Regards,

Debra Matteucci
Senior Editor & Editorial Coordinator
Harlequin Books
300 East 42nd Street
New York, NY 10017

Muriel Jensen

THE COMEBACK MOM

Harlequin Books

TORONTO • NEW YORK • LONDON
AMSTERDAM • PARIS • SYDNEY • HAMBURG
STOCKHOLM • ATHENS • TOKYO • MILAN
MADRID • WARSAW • BUDAPEST • AUCKLAND

ISBN 0-373-16654-0

THE COMEBACK MOM

Prologue

"Happy birthday to you! Happy birthday to you! Happy birthday, dear Liiibby..."

Libby Madison smiled as the off-key, out-of-tune but enthusiastic rendition of the old tune swelled around her. The wait staff of Truffles were gathered around the table like a cheerful white-coated, bow-tied army, and Charlene Whitney and Sara Perez, with whom she'd been coming to the restaurant every other Thursday night for ten years, smiled fondly at her as they sang. Other diners also picked up the chorus.

She tried to look worthy of their enthusiasm while feeling strangely disconnected from the proceedings.

She was thirty-five. God, that was ancient. She should have all the answers by now, shouldn't she? Or she should at least know the score. But she didn't—except to know that she was behind. It wasn't exactly that she was losing, but more as though the game had been called.

The young redheaded waiter who always saw that their table had extra focaccia bread, extra butter and extra whipped cream on their desserts offered, "And many moooore!" in a dramatic baritone. That was followed by cheers and applause that didn't cease until she blew out the candles.

There was more applause, then a distribution of plates, forks and cake, and she was left alone again with Charlene and Sara. A fire blazed behind them in a stone fireplace decorated with hunting horns, pewter mugs, bridle tack and other appointments intended to provide a European-country-inn atmosphere.

"When does the new book come out?" Sara asked, eyeing her square of cake as though it had the potential to hurt her. She was short and plump, and had been on a diet ever since Libby had met her in fifth grade. She lived in Lake Oswego with her lawyer husband, three children and a Saint Bernard, in what she seemed to consider suburban heaven.

Sara tossed her chin-length dark hair and picked up her fork, apparently resolved to indulge. The decision made, she smiled brightly. "I promised Molly we'd go to the autographing. She's hooked on *The Rosie Chronicles*. And, of course, she finds it all doubly exciting that the author is her aunt Libby."

Molly was seven, and though not Libby's biological niece, they had unofficially assumed a relationship. The child had all her mother's sweetness and all her lawyer father's balancing skepticism.

"Tell her I have the first one out of the box saved for her," Libby replied. "The signing's a week from Saturday at Hawthorne's at the mall."

"I suppose Boris Bumpkin will be there, hanging over your shoulder and basking in your celebrity?" Charlene's sarcastic question was asked as she forked a bite of cake. The dramatic redhead studied the sweet with the greedy interest she applied to everything, then placed it in her mouth with a seductive movement.

Charlene's credo was that a woman should always operate as though she were being observed by a wealthy, eligible man.

Libby frowned at her friend with annoyance mingled with understanding. Though very different, Libby and Charlene had something important in common—loneliness. Libby dealt with it by working long hours on her illustrations for the line of children's books that had gained her national attention. Charlene dealt with it by operating a lingerie boutique by day and touring singles bars by night, always on the lookout for the man who was handsome enough, rich enough, suave enough to be her husband.

There were even times when Libby secretly admired her. Charlene hadn't given up on finding Mr. Right. Libby had. The old saw was true. After a woman reached a certain age, every man she met was married, divorced and disillusioned, or single—for painfully obvious reasons.

Boris was one of the latter. Still, he was her friend.

"Boris *Pushkin*," Libby corrected, "and he's a very fine editor."

Charlene swallowed and rolled her eyes. "He's a nerd."

"Nerds," Libby said firmly, "are people, too. Just be quiet about him."

Charlene put her fork down and looked from Libby to Sara. "For heaven's sake, Lib. Don't you see a pattern here?"

Libby knew she'd missed something when Sara sighed, gave Charlene a speaking look and replied, "Yes, but let's not bring it up now, all right?"

"What pattern?" Libby demanded. "What are you talking about?"

"Your pattern with men. You use them to punish yourself."

At Libby's startled blink, Charlene shook her head. "Oh, not with a guy in leather or anything fun like that, but with every social misfit, every nerd, every wounded soul who isn't strong enough to deal with life and living."

Sara, too, put her fork down and pleaded, "Charlie, don't go there. It's her birthday."

"And she's thirty-five!" Charlene exclaimed with a horror that made it sound like "ninety-five!" "If she's ever going to get out of her studio and *live* her life, she has to forgive herself for not adopting the Bonello kids, and stop trying to make up for it by mothering this interminable line of men who act like children!"

Sara put a hand over her eyes and groaned. Libby pushed her cake away and dabbed at her mouth with her napkin.

Charlene drew a breath and squared her shapely shoulders. "I'm sorry, but it's time you look at yourself, before you turn around and discover you're fifty and still having *latte*s with Boris on Sunday afternoons. Savannah and Zachary are all grown up by now. Forget them."

Libby placed her napkin beside her plate and replied calmly, "I like Boris. Even if he isn't the paragon of charm and success you're searching for, he's a nice man."

Sara looked Libby in the eye apologetically. "Libby, he's a whiner who uses you like an audience."

"Then there was that sales rep," Charlene said, "who'd had his Major League career cut short. He got a year's worth of Wednesday-night dinners out of you."

"Bone spurs," Libby said stiffly, "at that age were a tragic—"

"He wasn't any good at the game," Sara interrupted mercilessly. "Remember? Tony checked up on him. He'd been cut from the team. His career ended abruptly because of his own lack of skill."

"Then there was the chef who got you to illustrate his cookbook and put him up in your coach house because he convinced you he'd lost everything in a fire. Then Tony found out he'd been axed from the Ritz and evicted from his apartment because of a tendency to tipple the sherry."

"He was recovering while we worked on the book."

"He wasn't recovering—he just didn't have money to buy booze."

Libby leaned back in her chair and confronted her friends. They weren't entirely wrong, but they weren't entirely right, either. Her tendency to befriend the underdog was a response to a need to nurture, not necessarily a need to make reparation for failing to keep the appointment with the Bonello family's lawyer.

She had been only twenty-five, after all, when she'd volunteered at the hospital the night four-year-old Savannah and five-month-old Zachary Bonello had been brought in, the only survivors of an automobile accident that had claimed their parents. Orphaned herself in high school, she'd been deeply touched by their plight and done her best to distract Savannah with stories while she and her baby brother spent several days in the hospital under observation.

During that time, John Miller, the Bonellos' attorney, had tried to find a family member willing to take in the children. But the only relative he'd been able to locate was an aunt in her eighties. She told him Mrs.

Bonello had a sister who'd left the family at age sixteen and never been heard from since. A very cold trail had led him to abort his attempt to find her. Seeing how attached Savannah had become to Libby, he'd teased that she should consider adopting the children.

But she'd been just getting by waitressing part-time while trying to market her illustrations. She'd given the matter serious thought, decided that it would be impossible to work full-time, pay a baby-sitter and still support herself and the children, much less pursue a career in art—then agreed to meet the attorney anyway to discuss the possibility. She could find a way to make it work. She knew she could.

She'd called an emergency meeting with Sara and Charlene at Truffles, told them what she was considering, and been told she was crazy. Sara had just married Tony then, and Charlene was trying to put the money together to buy her shop.

"How will you support two little children?" Sara had demanded.

"I'll find a way!" she'd said, completely determined that she would.

She'd practically lived at the hospital during the past few days, holding Savannah in her lap as the big-eyed child tried to right her overturned world.

She told her stories she'd written herself, and one she was trying to market, and read to her from the hospital's considerable children's library.

She fed Zachary and played with him, trying to make the room the children shared seem more like a home and less like a hospital room.

Savannah had asked her that morning when they'd be able to leave the hospital.

"Soon," she'd promised.

"Then, do we have to die and go to heaven?" she'd asked. "Or will we go live someplace else?"

The question had seemed logical to Savannah. Home was wherever her parents were, and Libby had been the one to explain carefully just two days before where Savannah's and Zachary's parents had gone.

That question had resolved her dilemma. The children needed an earthly mother and now. And she was sure they could adjust to living simply more easily than they could deal with the uncertainties of foster care.

She'd tried to explain that to her friends.

"What about your art?" Charlene had asked.

"It's my birthday," she'd told her with the certainty of a decision well made. "And that always feels like a fresh start. I can *do* this."

She'd left the restaurant enthused and excited, living in her imagination rather than paying attention to her surroundings—and been hit by a messenger on a bicycle. She'd awakened two days later in the hospital, a patient herself, to learn that a Bonello family friend had appeared and already taken the children away.

She'd felt as though she might die of disappointment and been tortured by images of Savannah wondering where she was and why she'd deserted her.

John Miller had assured her that the family friend was a fine, well-respected man and that the children would have better opportunities with someone in a stable financial position. On one level, she knew that to be true, but inside, she'd always felt as though things would have been different had she acted more decisively, more quickly. She'd inadvertently tampered with her own fate, botched her own karma.

Though she'd spent only four days with the children, she'd come to love them deeply. And the past ten years had seemed empty without them.

That sense of something unfinished that had plagued her since that fateful day seemed to inflate inside her.

"The children *aren't* all grown up." Wearily she corrected Charlene. "Savannah would be fourteen. Zachary would only be ten."

"It doesn't matter," Charlene insisted with a sympathetic touch on her arm. "They've belonged to someone else for ten years. *You're* all you've got, Libby. Do something about *you.*"

"She's got *us,*" Sara said, patting Libby's other arm. "Come on, Lib. Come home with me tonight. Tony's cousin from Boston is staying with us. He's a nice guy with a healthy podiatry practice, and if you discount a tendency to think he's king of karaoke, he can be fun."

Libby smilingly refused. "Thanks, but I'm on a deadline for Rosie's next adventure."

"Good grief. How many Rosie books will that make?" Charlene picked up her coffee cup with a graceful gesture and glanced around to see if anyone had noticed.

"Eleven," Sara replied.

"Thirteen." Libby pushed her wedge of cake aside and took a sip of coffee. "And my publisher doesn't seem to be getting tired of them."

"And he won't be as long as you keep winning the Caldicott Medal." Sara glanced at her watch and gasped. She hurriedly jammed the last bite of cake into her mouth, then reached for her purse. "I'm sorry, girls, but I've got to get home before Little Tony's ten o'clock feeding, or he'll make Big Tony's life miserable."

Charlene put her cup down and watched Sara's hurried preparations to leave. "Are you really that happy?" she asked. The question held less skepticism than genuine interest.

Sara stopped in the act of shrugging into a light wool jacket and looked back at her friend, clearly surprised that she'd asked. "Of course. Why?"

"Well, for one thing," Charlene replied, "if you were single and didn't have a man and three kids waiting for you, you could stay and have more coffee. You could party till the wee hours without being answerable to anyone."

Sara considered that but did not appear tempted. "Then I'd go to bed alone tonight, and there'd be no one to give me hugs and dandelions in the morning." She leaned down to hug Libby, then Charlene. "Happy birthday, Libby. Ignore us, okay? Do with your life what *you* want to do with it. God knows you've achieved more than either one of us."

Libby wondered about the truth of that as she and Charlene sat for another half hour, then settled the bill and waited just outside the door while the parking attendant went for their cars.

She'd made more money, had a big house in the hills, a Mercedes, and a personal trainer, but she hadn't borne any children as Sara had, and she hadn't maintained a belief in happily-ever-after as Charlene had.

"I didn't mean to sound like such a witch," Charlene said, staring moodily at the lights of Portland spread out before them like a sequined blanket. Then she turned to look into Libby's face, her eyes grave in the harsh light of the restaurant's doorway. "But you should find a *good* man. You have so much more to offer than I do. But they're not going to find *you* as long as you have losers hanging on to you. Please. Do yourself a favor. Forget what might have been with the children and live now—for you." She smiled suddenly and pointed to Libby's hair. "I like the new cut. Short is in, you know. It brings out your eyes and your cheekbones."

Libby accepted the compliment with an answering smile, but was thinking about Charlene's analysis. She doubted there was a man anywhere who didn't want mothering from a woman. Sara loved her Tony, but he often behaved like one of their children. And Charlene's men all used her and left her, displaying the selfish irresponsibility of narcissistic immaturity.

No. If she were to surround herself with family, she would add children, not a man.

Feeling as though she'd uncovered a grave truth, she said goodbye to Charlene as the driver brought up her Mercedes. She stepped out from behind the boxwood hedge that surrounded the restaurant and started across the driveway toward her car.

She wondered absently where the roar was coming from as she picked her way carefully over the decorative brick walk. Then she heard Charlene's shrill cry and saw the urgent expression on the attendant's face as he waved frantically at her. She stopped and turned as the sound grew louder. Mystified, she watched the bright glare of a single light approach her at great speed.

She tried to jump back, slipped, felt a painful blow to the back of her head and fell into a well of blackness.

Chapter One

Libby felt like a pressed cookie—as if she'd been stuffed into a tube, forced through a barbed opening and then baked. She was hot, bruised, and though she had yet to open her eyes, she knew that the single bright light that had knocked her down had somehow reshaped her.

Just before it struck her, she'd deduced that the light had been attached to the front of a bicycle. She remembered that her last thought before oblivion had been that she couldn't quite believe this could happen to someone twice in one lifetime. And in front of the same restaurant!

But it had, as the pain in every limb bore out.

She opened her eyes and blinked against the bright sunlight coming through the window. She focused on pale-green curtains, white acoustical ceiling tiles, a blank television screen perched on a shelf in a corner.

She groaned again. The hospital. Just like last time.

She moved arms and legs carefully, and was relieved to discover that although they caused her great pain, they did seem to be functioning. So she'd been lucky, just as she had been last time. Nothing broken.

She opened her eyes again, the sounds of quiet conversation filtering into the room as she continued to explore her surroundings. She noticed a smiling face drawn in red felt-tip pen on the wall just opposite the foot of the bed.

She frowned at that little detail. This must be the same room she'd occupied ten years ago. All hospital rooms did look alike, but she particularly remembered that smiley face. It amazed her that in ten years the housekeeping staff hadn't painted over it, or found a cleaner that would remove it.

At least, she thought bracingly, Doris Farthingale, the Gestapo-trained nurse who'd taken care of her ten years ago and who had terrified all the aides and volunteers, had been months from retirement back then. Maybe one of the younger nurses would still be here and they could reminisce.

"All right, look alive!" a husky voice said. She snatched Libby's wrist with all the delicacy of a lioness on the hunt and stared at her watch. "So, you're finally back. You've been in and out all night. Maybe we'll give you some breakfast."

It was the same voice. Not only that, those were the same words—verbatim—that she'd heard ten years ago.

No. That was impossible. Or coincidence. Certainly a nurse could choose to work beyond retirement—but ten years beyond it?

Libby eyed Farthingale as the nurse concentrated on her watch. She didn't look ten years older. Of course, middle-aged woman could look the same for a long period. But she thought she remembered that home-done perm in the process of growing out. It looked like a hairstyle Bozo would have been comfortable with.

Libby peered up into the same square face, saw the same no-nonsense, serviceable twitch of muscle that passed for a smile.

"Strong. Doctor's on his way to see you. Everything looks good, though you were out a couple of days. Hit your head on the brick walk. Soon as the doctor's finished, I'll let your friends in. They've been driving me crazy! Oh. And the nurses in Pediatrics said hello."

Libby felt gooseflesh break out on her scalp and along her arms as the nurse pushed the controls on the bed that placed her in a sitting position. This conversation was ten years old. But that *couldn't* be.

She thought back a decade, trying to remember what had happened next. She'd asked about the Bonellos. No. That had been later. First she'd asked what day it was.

"Doris?" she called as the woman pulled the door open.

Farthingale turned at the door as though surprised that Libby had deigned to interrupt her departure. "Yes?"

"What day is it, please?"

She knew the answer before it came and said the words to herself simultaneously. "Thursday. You slept through Wednesday."

Farthingale left the room.

All right. She wouldn't panic. There had to be an explanation. Maybe she was delusional. Maybe she was dreaming. Maybe... She smoothed her hair as she reflected, trying to calm herself, then conscious thought stopped abruptly. She could *see* her hair!

Goose bumps now broke out on her tongue and the soles of her feet.

Her hair was short now, not long enough to hang over her shoulder! Even Charlene had remarked on it just the night before—or two nights before—at her birthday dinner!

She put her hand to the straight, honey-blond ends resting on the front of her hospital gown at her breasts. The hair felt cool and silken against her fingertips. And very real. She touched her forehead and felt long bangs. This was no delusion and no dream.

Panic rising in her, she climbed gingerly out of bed and carefully covered the few steps to the bathroom at the end of the room. On the narrow wall was a mirror. Libby gasped at what she saw.

The reflection was hers, all right—just as she'd looked ten years before. Her face was a little rounder, her eyes a little more ingenuous. But how could this be! How *could* this be?

The doctor insisted that she was fine. She decided not to mention that she suspected she'd awakened this morning ten years back in time.

Had he been young and handsome, she might have slipped into the fictional possibilities of just such a scenario: he would understand her concern, be captivated by her beauty and her singular charm and help her sort through the facts and the clues to find out what had happened. Then he would marry her, move her into his home on Rock Creek Golf Course and buy her a Beamer that matched his.

But he was middle-aged and harried—just as he'd been ten years ago. He told her she would ache for several days, gave her a prescription for pain and advised her to lay low for a few days and to watch where she was going from now on.

Then Sara and Charlene came in to pick at her breakfast, help her dress and take her home. Sara was plump, newly married and probably pregnant with her first baby, Libby guessed.

Charlene looked fresh and bright, her mass of car-rotty hair caught back in a clip.

Libby let them scold her and bustle around her as Charlene told and retold the story of calling for an ambulance, riding with her to the hospital, phoning Sara and sitting in the waiting room for two days.

Libby dutifully raised her arms as Sara pulled her sweater over her head. She felt as though she were watching a movie she'd seen before. She knew the dialogue Charlene was about to tell her—that Truffles's manager had been by to see how she was.

"Mr. Wainwright from Truffles came by yesterday to see how you were doing," she said, fluffing Libby's hair as Libby emerged from the neck of the sweater.

Sara would tell her he felt responsible.

"He says he feels responsible, but Charlene saw the whole thing and that messenger was looking in his bag rather than watching where he was going. He should lose his license!"

Libby felt both an interest and a sort of distance from the goings-on. Even though she knew every line, she was unable to look away.

She was reliving her life! She'd lost the terror she'd felt earlier when she'd first realized what was happening. If she was indeed going around a second time, then she could relax, because she knew nothing horrible or monumental had happened in the past ten years, except that she'd achieved considerable success in her work. But she couldn't imagine why on earth it was happening—or what it meant!

"I'm sorry you were hurt," Charlene said, pushing her gently onto the bed and slipping her simple black pumps onto her feet, "but this might have been a blessing in disguise. I mean, there's no way you could have cared for those children and still—"

"Charlie!" Sara snapped at her.

Libby frowned from one to the other. The children. In the shock of her life's reprise, she'd forgotten them.

Then it hit her like a hammer. That was it! The Bonello children! Charlene was about to tell her that while she'd been unconscious the lawyer had left a message on her answering machine that a family friend had claimed the children.

She listened stoically as Sara began gently to explain.

"Charlie went to your apartment yesterday to make sure everything was okay—you know, that you hadn't left the iron on or anything. And while she was there, that lawyer called and left a message."

She hadn't asked what he'd said, sensing it was bad news.

"A family friend has claimed the children, Libby," Sara went on, just as she had then. "He's Savannah's godfather." She enfolded Libby in a long, firm hug. Then she'd pulled away, her own maternal heart in her eyes. "I know how disappointed you must feel, but you're going to be a great artist, meet a wonderful man and have beautiful, brilliant children of your own. Now, come on. We're going to take you home, I'm going to make you breakfast, and you're going to lie on the sofa and rest all day long."

She agreed, because she'd agreed ten years ago. Her friends drove her home.

She was fascinated, though not entirely surprised, when they took her to her small apartment rather than the hillside split level she'd bought when Rosie had gained national attention and earned her a new publishing contract in the high six figures.

Charlene tucked her under a blanket on the sofa, while Sara fixed scrambled eggs and toast. They pulled kitchen chairs up beside her and ate off their laps and made plans for the future with false cheer.

It was bizarre, she thought, to look into the fresh young faces of her friends and know exactly what had become of their hopes, ten years later—that Sara would experience all the happiness with Tony that she foresaw, and that Charlene would have her shop but that she was facing a long search for the man of her dreams.

She shooed them away when they promised to stay with her the rest of the day.

"I'll be fine," she insisted, waving her cordless phone at them just as she'd done ten years before. "If I need anything, I promise to call."

"I took the day off work so I could be with you," Sara said.

"Then spend it making something wonderful for dinner. Tony would love that." She sat up and smiled brightly, trying to look well on the road to recovery. "And you have a Western Civ class this afternoon, don't you?" she asked Charlene.

"I can skip once," Charlene shouted over her shoulder as she carried kitchen chairs back to the table.

"I thought this was finals week."

"I arranged to take a makeup."

"Now you don't have to. I'm fine. Go, both of you. I promise I'll call if I need the least little thing."

They'd protested but they'd gone, just as they had ten years ago. Or now. She had to stop thinking about this as ten years ago because it was now even though she'd done it all ten . . . before.

It was all too confusing. All she was beginning to conclude for certain was that this could only be happening because something in the past had to be repaired. Wasn't that what always motivated the voyager in movies that dealt with time travel?

Or was that restless spirits?

She guessed if she had a choice between having been moved around in time and having actually crossed over, she'd gratefully accept what had happened.

And because she'd come to love Savannah and Zachary so much, she had no doubt at all why she was here—to get them back.

Now came the tricky part. So far, everything had gone just as it had ten years . . . the first time. The same words had been spoken, the same small details accomplished.

But the first time, she'd stayed on the sofa and cried her heart out.

This time, she was going to endeavor to repair the past, but would the otherworldly conditions that had led her back to this time allow that? Had she come to the correct conclusion? Would she be allowed to get up off the sofa, or would she be held to the events as they'd occurred the first time?

She tossed the blanket back, stood and waited for some invisible hand to push her back. It didn't. She walked to the telephone and dialed the attorney's number, perching on the edge of the telephone table while the line rang, crossing one leg over the other.

Was she imagining it, or did she feel particularly buoyant and agile? Was this some user-friendly parallel universe in which she would find herself more comfortable than she'd been before?

Miller's secretary connected her.

"Elizabeth!" the attorney said, his tone concerned. "Are you all right? I'm so sorry about the accident."

She smiled. Those were the first words since she'd awakened that morning that she hadn't heard before. She'd turned a new page, moved into a new phase of the past. She frowned for a moment over the notion that that was even possible, then put it aside.

If she was to go on with righting the past, she had to stop worrying about just where it was and simply live it.

"I'm bruised but fine, John," she replied. "Your message said that a family friend has claimed the children."

"Yes." His tone was apologetic. "I'm sorry there wasn't a better way to tell you, but when I left the message I didn't know you'd been in an accident, and you were expected at my office the evening before. When you didn't come, I thought you'd changed your mind. Until your friend heard my message and called to tell me what had happened to you."

"I know, it's no one's fault. It was just one of those strange quirks of fate, I guess." A little shudder bumped up her spine as she said the words. Quirk, indeed. "Can you tell me about the family friend? He didn't come to see the children at the hospital."

She heard the rustle of papers on the other end of the line.

"No. Seems he'd been to Scotland on business, then went fishing in the wilds with a friend. They put themselves deliberately out of reach for a few days, never suspecting, I'm sure, that such a tragedy would occur. Anyway, as soon as he heard, he flew right back. He's an architectural historian who now runs a kind of architectural salvage business."

Libby wrinkled her nose, though there was no one to see the gesture. Architectural historian. That sounded fogeyish. Poor children. And it intensified her sense of rightness about her mission. She'd definitely been sent back in time to rescue those children from the dreary prospect of life with an academic.

"Does he live here in Portland?" she asked hopefully.

"No, on the Long Beach Peninsula in Washington. He's taking the children there tomorrow."

Libby stood and squared her shoulders, determined that it was time to begin building her case for her guardianship of the children.

"You're sure he's qualified to care for the children?" she asked. "I mean, doesn't there have to be some legal procedure—"

"He's planning to adopt, of course," Miller replied. "Ransom is Savannah's godfather. As young parents the Bonellos probably felt pretty invincible and didn't bother to draw up wills, but I checked Ransom's claim with church records and it's valid. And Children's Services seems quite satisfied with him. They've even agreed to let him take the children out of state pending the final decree. As I said, he lives on the Long Beach Peninsula in Washington. There'll be a few visits from a caseworker, but I'm sure his adoption of the children will be uncontested." There was a moment's pause, then he added quietly, "I know you grew fond of the children, Libby, but I promise you I wouldn't put them into a situation I felt at all uncertain about."

Libby's new buoyancy evaporated with that news. But *she* was supposed to assume their care. Wasn't that why she was brought back? Wasn't that why *not* having them had haunted her for ten years?

"John...I didn't get to say goodbye to the children," she said, trying to remain calm. "Would you tell me where they are?"

Another pause. "With him," he answered finally. "They're spending the night at the Rockland. The presidential suite. But, Libby..."

Hmm. The presidential suite? A fogey with a taste for the good life. "Thank you, John," she said, and hung up.

Libby showered, washed her hair and tried to pin it up for a mature look, but quickly changed her mind when the bruise at the back of her head ached in response.

She was surprised to open her closet and find her clothes comfortingly familiar, but then, all she wore were classic casual slacks and sweaters, and she never discarded anything that was comfortable, no matter how old it was.

She pulled on butternut-colored woolen slacks, a moss-green sweater that she accented with a paisley scarf in earth tones, and topped the look with a slouchy velvet hat the same color as the sweater. She checked her reflection in the mirror, and decided she looked about fourteen.

She pushed her hair up into the hat, unrolled the brim and stepped back for a critical appraisal. Now she looked eighty.

She pulled off the hat, went back to the closet and snatched a small brown tweed close-fitting hat off the shelf. It boasted a long, swept-back plume secured to the right side with a jeweled pin. She held her bangs back and fitted the hat low on her forehead.

It didn't hide her long hair, but it did give her an air of eccentricity and maturity. The last thing she wanted was for the fogey to think he was dealing with an insecure young woman with limited prospects and an uncertain look in her eye.

She squared her shoulders. So she'd had a confrontation with a bicycle and been tossed ten years into the past. She was determined to be in charge of her present—wherever—whenever—that was.

She grabbed her purse. That, too, was familiar, and all she'd ever carried since Sara and Charlene had given it to her when she'd graduated from the Museum School. It was soft brown leather and large enough to hold a sketch pad, as well as everything else essential to her peace of mind.

She laughed a little hysterically at the blue Toyota in her driveway, then climbed into it, dismissing the Mercedes convertible from her mind. It was out there somewhere, ten years into her future, and she had to make do with the Celica she'd bought used when she'd graduated.

She wondered idly as she headed for the freeway and downtown what getting the children from the fogey would do to the future. Wouldn't a station wagon be more appropriate to her life than the Mercedes?

Well, that was a problem for a later date. Right now, she had to concentrate all her energies into convincing the fogey that she would be a more suitable parent for Savannah and Zachary. If she was lucky, he'd even be grateful that someone else was willing to assume responsibility. After all, if his business took him to places like Scotland, having two little children around could prove a major inconvenience.

Yes. That would be a good argument.

IT WAS two o'clock in the afternoon when she knocked
on the door of the Rockland Hotel's presidential suite.
The cacophonous sounds of shouting adults and
screaming children could be heard beyond the door.

Then it was yanked open as a small mustachioed man
in a three-piece suit marched through it, pushing her
aside with an abrupt and ill-tempered "pardon me."

He turned to confront the tall man who appeared in
the doorway in his wake. On the tall man's left arm was
Zachary Bonello, and it was easy to tell that the baby
was desperately upset about something. His cheeks were
apple red, his eyes screwed shut and his little mouth
wide open and emitting screams at jumbo-jet takeoff
levels.

"I know they've been crying for hours!" the man
holding Zachary shouted after the smaller man, "and
as soon as I figure out how to stop them, I will. But
considering what you charge for this room, and considering there are no other guests on this floor, I'm surprised you can't be a little more tolerant."

"I'm sorry, sir," the little man said stiffly, "but we've
had complaints from guests on the *ground* floor. You
must do something about the noise, or we'll have to ask
you to leave."

The little man stalked away, and Libby found herself
face-to-face with the tall man, who looked as though the
wrong word could push him to murder.

He turned the baby onto his shoulder, patted his back
a little awkwardly and shouted at her over his screams.
"I know, I know! You've paid good money for a
peaceful, quiet room, and you're not getting it. I understand. But help is on the way. Please be patient."

In jeans and a chambray shirt, he looked down on
Libby with an air of exasperated desperation she might

have smiled at if it hadn't been so important that she get on his good side. He must be employed by the fogey, in which case it was important that she win him over. Her future was at stake here, and that of the children.

She gauged his amenability. The man was big shouldered and lean hipped, with the angular face and smoky dark eyes one often saw under the brim of a Stetson on the cover of a country-music album. Was he some assistant architectural historian? Some associate fogey?

She smiled tentatively and reached both hands out for the baby. "May I?" she asked.

He gazed at her doubtfully. "I don't think so. Everybody from the maid to the elevator operator has tried to—"

She lifted the baby from his arms, smug with her insider knowledge that this particular infant was colicky and had responded well in the hospital to the football hold. She rested him on his stomach on the flat of her hand and patted his back. His sobs quieted almost immediately to sniffs and breathy gulps.

The man was astounded. She smiled modestly.

"I was looking for Jared Ransom," she said, trying to see past him into the room. But he filled the doorway.

His eyes moved from the baby to her face, roved it with a thoroughness that made her wonder if he was analyzing her facial architecture, then rose to the feather on her hat and lingered there for a moment of apparent indecision.

She noticed, while he was distracted by her plumage, that his eyes were thickly lashed and very dark.

Then he lowered them to hers and said, his voice reflecting mild confusion, "I'm Jared Ransom. And you are?"

She clenched her teeth to prevent her jaw from dropping. Then she had to think about the question while her mind tried to adjust to the difference between her image of Jared Ransom and the reality. The fogey was gorgeous.

She forced her brain into gear again. He was still single, with a job that took him out of the country. And he did not seem to be dealing well with at least one of the children. She would be better for them than he would.

She began to give him her name, when a light seemed to go on in his eyes and he said with sudden relief, "Of course! You must be from Northwest Nannies. I appreciate your coming so promptly."

Libby opened her mouth to correct his misconception, then stopped when she recognized that moment as significant. She could tell him the truth as she'd intended. Or she could accept his misinterpretation of her presence as the gift it was—just as the trip back in time was—just as the opportunity to spend time with the children would be.

In light of what had happened to her since she'd opened her eyes that morning, it seemed entirely possible that this was a present from the hand of God Himself, ordained to rectify the past.

With a sense of free-falling without a rip cord within reach, she smiled widely and offered her hand. "Elizabeth Madison," she said. "Libby."

He shook her hand in a warm, firm grip, then resumed his earlier frown as he pulled her inside. "Come on in. I have a second challenge for you inside."

Libby got a quick impression of blue-and-ivory silk wallpaper and Queen Anne furnishings as Jared led the way through the small living area to a large room beyond. It was a bedroom.

He swept a large, square hand to the king-sized sleigh bed covered in a pink-and-green flowered quilt. "Let's see what you can do with that," he said.

She studied it a moment, her mind sorting through all the possible interpretations of the statement. She turned to him, an eyebrow raised.

He returned her look blandly for a moment, then quickly shook his head. "No. *Under* the bed. Savannah—your second charge—has been under the bed since breakfast."

"Oh." Libby laughed softly and handed him back the baby, taking his muscled arm and making a hook of it so that the baby could remain on its stomach. Then she got down on her hands and knees and peered under the bed skirt.

"Savannah?" she called. "Hi, baby. It's Libby."

There was a little squeal, followed by the sounds of a rapid crawl. Then a small, round-faced little girl with large, tear-filled brown eyes and disheveled brown braids burst from under the bed and into her arms.

The child clutched a foot-high handmade doll designed to replicate a gingerbread man. It had black button eyes, was trimmed in white rickrack, and the nap of its fabric was balding in spots from being held. Libby remembered that Savannah had been clutching the doll when she'd been brought into the hospital.

Libby sat back on her heels and simply held her, knowing she'd been right about why she'd been sent back here. The children needed her. They *wanted* her.

And she wanted them. Now all she had to do was explain that to Jared Ransom.

She hugged Savannah to her with one hand and pushed herself to her feet with the other. She turned to see Ransom right beside her, his frown suspicious.

"You *know* these children?" he demanded.

Chapter Two

Libby felt an instant's panic, then realized the true answer was both reasonable and safe to give. "I volunteer in Pediatrics at the hospital. I read to the children."

He studied her a moment then seemed to relax, apparently finding it logical that a young nanny would volunteer her spare time to care for sick children.

She became even more convinced that divine intervention was at work here.

JARED WAS DOING his best to keep his head despite the unreality of the past few days. He'd lost the man who'd been a lifelong friend, the woman who'd been the love of his life, and he'd assumed guardianship of their two children, when he knew next to nothing about how to care for them.

Then, in his darkest hour, this plumed angel appeared and hushed the tumult in his world. It was weird. He'd always felt that things that seemed too good to be true generally were.

But she seemed to be true. She was certainly flesh and blood. Pink and smooth flesh that was just a little freckled over a small, straight nose. She had summer-sky eyes, a berry colored mouth and long, straight hair the color of old marble. And that incredible package was topped by a tweed hat with a preposterous feather.

Her appearance had a sort of magical effect on a situation he'd begun to believe was hopeless. Now, after eighteen hours of one child screaming and the other hiding, both were quiet and a new serenity was settling over his surroundings.

A subtle disturbance stirred inside him where he usually managed to maintain clarity and peace. A beautiful nanny appearing at just the right moment and seeming to be precisely what the children needed? Was he trapped in a television sitcom, or had heaven sent him an angel?

His eyes went to the feather on her hat as he lingered over the thought.

"I want my mommy," Savannah wept pathetically against Libby's neck. "I want my daddy!"

The child had been telling him that for the past eighteen hours. He had no idea how to explain to a four-year-old that her parents were dead and that she would never see them again.

Libby glanced up at him, her eyes filled with empathy. "Has she eaten?"

He shook his head. "Not a bite today."

"Would you see if room service can deliver a grilled cheese and a glass of milk?"

"Sure." Jared took the baby into the other room and called room service. While waiting for them to pick up, he heard Libby's voice soothing Savannah.

"We talked about this in the hospital, remember? Mommy and Daddy went to heaven to be with God."

"I want them to come back!"

"They can't, sweetie. Now it's just us, but we're going to be fine. You'll see."

Just us. Jared leaned a hip against the back of the sofa, the baby now sound asleep on his forearm, and thought her "us" had a particularly intimate sound, as though he'd been left out of it.

He concluded the next moment that that was ridiculous. It was just that *he* felt far less competent with the children than she obviously was. Then room service answered and he turned his attention to placing the order.

While Libby and Savannah ate on stools at a small bar that separated a tiny kitchen from the living area, Jared put the sleeping baby in his carrier. Then he braced himself and called his mother. Everything had happened so fast that he hadn't had a chance yet to tell her about Frank and Mandy and his impulsive decision to take the children.

He was grateful when he got his mother's answering machine. He simply told her he was finally back in the country and that he'd be home the following afternoon.

She wasn't going to like this. Though she was always campaigning for him to marry and produce grandchildren, she wouldn't be happy that he'd chosen to connect himself forever with the children of the woman who'd left him for his best friend.

He felt as though he'd resolved the past, but his mother was fiercely loyal to him. She thought of Mandy only in the darkest terms.

Now all he had to figure out was how in the hell he was going to do this. He was certain that he'd figure it out eventually; his business life was all about salvage, after all, and he was good at it.

He went to the counter in the kitchen, where room service had left the tray, and poured himself a cup of coffee. He turned to find two pairs of eyes on him—one pair wide and dark and frightened, the other clear blue and speculative.

Libby had taken off her hat, and gold bangs skimmed her eyebrows, while the lustrous length of her hair lay like a shawl around her shoulders and down her back. For a moment, he was helpless to pull his eyes away from it.

Then Savannah squirmed and he turned his attention to her. He noticed that she'd eaten half the sandwich and pushed the rest away. Her small fingers were wrapped around the glass of milk, and she sported a white mustache.

"Scooby is on," she said, as though the statement required some action on his part.

He didn't even know what Scooby was, or what it was on and why that created a problem for a four-year-old.

"It's a cartoon," Libby explained, her tone a little superior, he thought. " 'Scooby-Doo.' On television."

"Ah." He pointed to the set, relieved to be faced with an issue he could actually do something about. "Go ahead and turn it on."

Savannah immediately scrambled off the stool.

"When she's settled," he said, stopping Libby as she turned to follow the child, "you and I should discuss a few things. I'll be making some calls in the bedroom."

She nodded. "I'll find you."

He watched Libby detour to check on Zachary, still comfortably asleep in his carrier on the coffee table, then get comfortable with Savannah in a corner of the sofa. The child's little legs stuck straight out in front of her, her tiny tennis shoes protruding from a pair of jeans trimmed in daisies. Libby gracefully crossed her legs and hooked an arm around the little girl, who leaned into her.

She seemed perfect. She'd been here under an hour and already a pretty desperate situation was under control. He just had the most unsettling feeling that control was in her hands and not his.

He sat at the round table near the window and punched up the telephone book on his laptop. He called Columbia Freight and discovered that his shipment from Scotland would arrive the following Monday, so he'd have a few days to make room for it in his workshop. Then he called his client for the Corinthian columns and listened to twenty minutes of her raptures on the garden house she intended to build around them.

"*Please* watch for a stone urn," she said. "Wouldn't that just complete the interior with cascading ivy?"

"I think my mother has one in her shop," he said. "It's just a molded concrete pot, but there's an architectural sculpture of three angels back to back coming with my shipment. It'd be a great spot to put the urn."

"Perfect! Call me when it comes."

He phoned his brother.

"King's Ransom," Darren's cheerful bass voice answered. In the background could be heard the sounds of pots and pans and the din of a busy kitchen.

"An anchovy-and-pineapple pizza, please," Jared ordered gravely, "and a side of curly fries. Could you deliver that?"

"Do they let you eat," Darren asked, "in the orthopedic unit of the hospital?"

Jared grinned to himself. "You're not suggesting that you can put me there?"

Darren lowered his voice. "After four days of Mom visiting me, I could tie the Eiffel Tower in a knot! Where the hell are you?"

"Portland," Jared replied on a low laugh. "I'll be home tomorrow. You're such a wuss. Mom visits *me* all the time."

"*You* have ten acres and several buildings to get lost in!" Darren's angry whisper was growing more desperate. "*I* live in a four-room condo, three rooms of which are now occupied by our mother and the dogs. And that includes the kitchen and the bathroom. If I want to eat or... read, I have to do it at the restaurant."

Jared could sympathize. His mother had three of the most annoying dogs on the face of the planet. "What's she doing there?"

"I'm not sure."

"What do you mean, you're not sure?"

"I mean, I'm not the confidant you are. She just settled for me because *you* were in Scotland. What, please God, can you do in Scotland that you can't do here?"

"Buy the contents of a castle."

There was silence on the other end of the line while Darren apparently considered the irrefutability of that, then he sighed audibly. "Besides that," he groused.

"Buy you a case of the smoothest scotch you've ever tasted."

Another silence while Darren wondered whether or not to believe him. "Did you really?"

"Yes."

"Thank you." Darren's voice became suddenly conciliatory. "Now, if you'll get Mom out of my place, I'll only break one of your legs."

"Well..." He didn't know how to tell him that his mother was the last person he needed to see at the moment.

"Oh, no," Darren barked. "I don't care if you have brought home a delicious Scottish lass, my sanity is more important than your sex life."

"You don't have any sanity."

"And you have more sex in your life than the NFL, so help me out here!"

Calmly, quietly, Jared told his brother about Frank and Mandy's deaths. "I just happened to call his office from Edinburgh because I'd found a partner's desk he'd always wanted, and heard about the accident. I hurried right back."

"I'm sorry. I know how much he meant to you." Darren sighed. "And I know you never stopped loving her."

"That was a long time ago."

"Yeah." The simple affirmative lacked conviction. "So, do you have to settle the estate or something?"

That was certainly one way of putting it. "They left two children," he said. "I've got them."

There was another heavy pause. "For how long?"

"Until they go away to college, I imagine."

A choke. "You're kidding me, right?"

"No. I have a four-year-old girl in the living room of my hotel suite at this very moment, watching cartoons, and a five-month-old boy fast asleep in a carrier."

"Jared—" Darren began.

"I know," Jared cut him off quietly. He realized how difficult it was going to be. He didn't have to have it pointed out. "Frank and I were friends since college, and Mandy... well..." There were no words for what Amanda Breen had meant to him. "Anyway, tell Mom

I said hi and that I'm going to need a little time to get the kids settled in and establish a routine.''

"By yourself?" Darren sounded incredulous.

"Relax. I've hired a nanny." Jared looked up as he spoke the words, and found that Libby stood in the doorway. She backed away when she saw he was on the phone, but he beckoned her to return, and pointed to the chair opposite him.

"Darren, I've got to go," he said. "Don't worry. Tell Mom, but don't let her worry, and I'll call both of you as soon as we're settled in."

"But..."

He hung up on his brother's protest.

LIBBY MADE HERSELF relax in her chair while trying to deal with the facts she'd overheard. He had a mother and a sibling—she hadn't been able to determine male or female by his end of the conversation—and he intended to keep the children until they went away to college.

Well. That certainly put her in a more difficult position than she'd anticipated. She'd hoped his experience with them today would have made him susceptible to a subtle suggestion on her part that he might not be cut out for the role of parent.

But he'd sounded resolved on the phone. And he seemed to have valid reasons for having made his decision. Apparently the children's father had been his best friend. And their mother. Libby didn't know what the connection was there, except that she'd heard something in his voice when he'd said her name.

That would be interesting to speculate about, but the issue at the moment was the children.

"Zachary still asleep?" Jared Ransom asked her.

"Yes," she replied. "And Savannah's asleep on the sofa."

"Good." He leaned into the back of his chair and stretched long legs out to the side. "I was beginning to think I'd never get her out from under the bed. Lucky you came so quickly after my call."

She answered with a smile. A lie of omission had to be less evil than the real thing, she felt sure.

"This is going to be a big job, Mr. Ransom," she suggested in a tone that she hoped sounded respectful without being patronizing.

Apparently it didn't come off. He raised an arrogant eyebrow. "I thought you handled the children very competently," he replied.

She felt off balance for an instant. "I meant it'll be a big job for you," she corrected.

He nodded, folding his hands over a flat stomach. His eyes were reading her. She didn't like that, but she met them intrepidly.

"I'd figured that out, Libby," he said. "But it's something I'm determined to do. So I will. I wanted to talk about *your* role in my household."

Her role. For ten years she'd seen her role as the children's mother. Only she'd botched it. Now that she had a second chance, she wasn't going to blow it again.

"I can care for them, of course." She spoke quietly, carefully. "But I can't replace a parent's love and understanding."

"I'm not asking you to," he said, a slight pleat between his eyebrows. "I will provide the love and understanding as soon as I figure out how it's done. I—"

"But you have no experience with children, have you?"

"I'd say that was mercilessly obvious. I'm used to dealing with wood and marble and plaster—heavy, substantial things. The children are so small and fragile that they terrify me. But I'll get over it. Other men seem to."

Libby found that admission disarmingly frank. It compounded her feeling of being off balance. "You travel a lot, don't you?" she said, then realized her gaffe. "My boss...mentioned it," she added quickly, praying that he'd shared that information when he'd called the nanny service.

His gaze pinned her for a long moment. She expected him to spring to his feet, declare her a fraud and order her out of his suite and out of their lives.

She held his stare, everything inside her poised for battle. But he nodded after a moment and smiled politely. "I take several trips a year. That's why I requested a nanny who could move to Washington with us and travel if need be. Are you willing to relocate?"

She barely bit back a smile. She'd moved ten years back in time. A hundred miles into another state hardly seemed a challenge.

She wondered if it wouldn't be much simpler just to blurt out the truth. *Look, Ransom. I fell in love with these children while you were chasing whatever kind of fish lives in Scotland, and frankly, though your most outstanding qualities are great good looks and an ability to melt diamonds with your eyes, I don't see that they'll do you much good as a parent, so why don't you drop the whole idea of becoming a bachelor father and let me do what God sent me back to do. Let me have these children.*

But something in his eyes told her that despite his quiet, controlled manner, no business conducted with this man would go easily for the second party. He'd just told her he was used to dealing with wood, marble and plaster—all hard substances. She guessed that somewhere along the way he'd acquired some of their properties.

"I can relocate," she said, "but I have a particular affection for these children because . . . because I got to know them in the hospital. I just wonder how wise it is to uproot them when their little worlds are already upside down and—"

"Elizabeth."

Her father used to say her name in just that way. There was a kind of reckoning in the tone, a reminder that one of them was parent and one child—or in this case, employer and employee.

"Let's clarify something here," he said. "I don't usually explain myself to anyone, but I understand that your position as nanny creates a unique situation and I have to consider that. But while the daily care of the children would be yours, the responsibility for their welfare, their sense of security, even Savannah's recovery from the loss of her parents, is mine. I am not hiring you to pass that on to you. Frank Bonello was my best friend since college, and his wife and I were . . . acquainted . . . before she ever met him."

Libby speculated over the word he'd chosen so carefully, but she remained still as he went on.

"Now, that isn't your business, but I'm telling you only so that you'll understand how serious I am about this. Those children are the offspring of my best friend and a woman I never stopped . . . caring about, and they have no one else in the world but me. I intend to love them and raise them and am perfectly prepared for it to be difficult for me." He sighed, as though explaining all that had been a chore. "I hoped that hiring a nanny would make the adjustment less difficult for the children. But a nanny who doubts my abilities isn't going to be good for any of us. I'll be happy to pay you for today and ask the agency to send someone else. I'll even tell them you found us unsuitable rather than the other way around."

He waited for an answer.

Libby fought desperately to keep thinking while dealing with panic. She couldn't let him dismiss her! Not only would that immediately separate her from the children, but when he called the agency to replace her and discovered they hadn't sent her, she'd be in trouble big time. And the story of how she insinuated herself into Jared's hotel room was sure to make her look completely insane and unscrupulous.

It also would not please a judge if she ended up in court one day, fighting Jared for custody of the children.

So, she had to make this plan work so that it wouldn't come to that.

"Please," she said, trying to quiet the flutter in her voice. The way she saw it, she had no alternative but to swallow her pride, apologize for presuming too much, and agree to hire on. Raising two little children was going to be harder for him than even he imagined. Her only recourse was to be around when it all fell apart on him and he finally gave up. Then they would be hers. "You're right, of course. I'm sorry. I'm a little... over-eager, I guess. I'd like to stay on and help." She looked at him directly with as much dignity as she could muster. "Unless you'd like to replace me."

He held her gaze, then after an interminable moment, sighed and shook his head. "No. You deal well with the children, and Savannah seems very fond of you—that will help. I was thinking you'd work five days a week, have weekends off unless I'm away, then you'd get compensating time off." Then he proposed a monthly salary that was more than she made in three months waitressing—with tips.

"That sounds . . . satisfactory," she said.

"Good." He stood. She followed. "Can you pack your things and make your arrangements and be back tonight?"

She looked worried. "Will you be all right until then?"

"If you hurry."

Libby rode to the ground floor in the elevator, thinking wryly that the trip back in time may have been a gift, but it was beginning to look a little like a Trojan horse.

On her way through the lobby, she heard a young woman in a severe suit ask for Jared Ransom's room. She intercepted her before the desk clerk could put through a call.

"Are you from . . . ?" What had he called it? "Northwest Nannies?"

The girl was probably college age, and wore glasses, no makeup and a very grave expression. When she nodded, Libby hooked an arm in hers and walked her back toward the door, explaining that she was Jared Ransom's secretary and that the position of nanny had been filled.

The girl smiled thinly. "Good. I wanted a placement in Southern California anyway."

Libby thanked heaven for the ease with which she'd been able to handle that obstacle, and headed for her car.

JARED STOOD at the living-room window and watched the gold-colored speck six floors down that was Libby Madison run across the street to the parking lot.

He didn't know what to make of her. He could look at almost any antique object in a home, from plumbing fixtures to garden ornaments, date it within a few years, set a value on it and explain its history to a client.

But the nanny had him puzzled. Something about her seemed curiously out of line or tune or sync. He didn't know which or why. But she was good with the children, and he was more desperate for help with them than he wanted her to know.

Becoming a single parent was nothing he would have chosen to do, but he owed his friend, and his first thought yesterday when he'd looked into Savannah's eyes was that she should have been his. And now she was. And so was Zachary. And if the quirky nanny helped make that possible, it wasn't important that he understand her. He just had to take her with them to Cranberry Harbor.

LIBBY HELD the baby in one arm and Savannah by the hand as her new employer hauled suitcases out of the back of the truck he'd left at the Portland Airport when he'd flown to Scotland. The day was overcast and cold, and she felt Savannah huddle against her side as she stared at Jared Ransom's house.

It stood on a broad expanse of sand and sea grass between the Pacific Ocean and a two-lane highway that led farther down the peninsula. Tall, long-needled pines hovered protectively near it, and a fence with alternating tall and shorter pickets the same gray-green color of the house surrounded a struggling lawn. To the side beyond the fence was one large shedlike structure on which the name ARCHI-JUNK had been painted in tall, green letters.

But it was the structure of the house itself that claimed her attention. It was two storied, with three tall peaks, a deep veranda and a decorative trim along the peaks and roofline that appeared delicate enough to be made of lace. That was impossible, she knew, but the work was so fine it gave an appearance of softness to the sharp angles.

Jared joined her and the children.

"Is that Gothic architecture?" she asked as he left the lineup of bags where they were and led the way up the steps.

"The details are Gothic, but the style is called Original American." He inserted a key in the lock, pushed the door open and gestured her inside. "Go on in. I'll bring the bags up."

Savannah, clutching her gingerbread doll, kept pace with her as she moved into a high-ceilinged living room that was surprisingly light and airy, given the seriousness of the lines of the house. The walls were white, and a wide, scrolly wood trim was a warmer ecru shade. A big, comfortable-looking sofa was upholstered in a big blue-and-white check and placed at an angle to what appeared to be a blue marble-trimmed fireplace. The mantel, she noticed in fascination, was hand-painted with a scene depicting a colonial house and a spotted horse. She knew nothing about antiques, but got the feeling it was very old.

A love seat in the same check fabric squared off the area around the fireplace, and a winged-back chair in red, white and blue stood off a ways under a standing Tiffany lamp.

Ecru draperies were open at all the windows, and a deep window seat across the room drew Savannah's attention. She went to it and climbed up to sit among the red, white and blue cushions.

Comfort seemed to have been combined with probably costly antiques to create an atmosphere that was both welcoming and awe inspiring.

"A logger built this in 1896," Jared said as he dropped the last bag inside and closed the door behind him. He looked around with a satisfied nod. "It's been through a few hands since then. I bought it five years ago when I came home again."

"From where?" she asked, interested, then remembered that he'd drawn the line last night between himself and her. She was the nanny. His past was none of her business.

"The East Coast," he replied easily.

Which surprised her. Apparently he didn't feel that revealing that much blurred the line.

"I'd spent a few years helping restore a Georgian mansion in Maryland, and a Victorian in Connecticut. Did I mention I'm an architectural historian?"

She opened her mouth to admit that Miller had told her, then remembered she wasn't supposed to know him. She pretended surprise, instead. "What does that involve?"

"It used to mean helping restore historic homes and buildings, but now I'm into the lighter side of it. I save architectural details from buildings that are being torn down or renovated, restore them in the workshop you probably noticed as we came in . . ."

She nodded.

"Then I have a shop in town where I sell them to people looking for something interesting and different."

She had to admit to herself that that didn't sound fogeyish at all.

"It must be exciting to tie into the past that way. Did you ever feel . . ." She hesitated, not entirely sure what she meant to ask: Did he ever feel as though *he'd* been caught in the past? Even only ten years past? "You know, sort of . . . connected?"

His brow furrowed at the question even as he smiled. "If you mean, have I come upon any ghosts, the answer is no. But I have sometimes run my hand along a banister, or stood in the middle of a mirrored ballroom and felt . . ." Then he hesitated and his expression grew more serious as he struggled to explain. "I don't know . . . energy, laughter, passion . . . leftover, I guess, because it was just too strong to die with whoever had felt it."

Yes. She understood. Love for the children had brought her back.

The baby began to fuss, and the sudden tension evaporated in the need to warm a bottle and find the baby food she'd stashed in the diaper bag.

Jared led the way to a large kitchen, with tall, old-fashioned cupboards painted forest green and up-to-the-minute stove, refrigerator, dishwasher and microwave disguised behind facades of oak bead board. A long, wide oak table occupied the middle of the room, and eight paddle-backed chairs were pulled up to it.

The wall above the stove held several plank shelves that bore decoys, old tins, a clay crock and a large painting of a garlic bulb.

A lacy, three-tiered bird cage hung from an exposed beam in the center of the room.

Libby stared until Zachary's distress galvanized her into action. She zapped rice cereal briefly in the microwave and poured in milk they'd stopped for on the way home.

While she settled in one of the captain's chairs to feed the baby, Jared looked through the cupboards to find something for lunch.

"Vegetable soup?" he asked Savannah.

She stood at Libby's side. "Yucky," she said with quiet disapproval.

"Okay." He held the door of the cupboard open farther as he perused its contents. "Tuna?"

"No."

"Peanut butter?"

"No."

He turned from the cupboard, a teasing smile in place. "Artichoke hearts?"

Savannah turned frowningly to Libby. "What's that?"

Libby laughed. "I don't think you'd like them. Why don't we have the soup?"

Savannah considered that, then wandered from Libby's chair to stand beside Jared and strain up on tiptoe to look for herself. "I can't see," she complained.

Jared held his hands down to her. "Want a boost up?"

She studied him suspiciously for a moment, then raised her arms.

He scooped her up and rested her on his hip. She grabbed a fistful of the sleeve of his gray-and-blue plaid flannel shirt and peered among the boxed and canned goods.

She pointed victoriously. "Olives!" she said.

Jared looked into the bright-brown eyes, at the wisps of brown hair escaping the braids Libby had recombed that morning and the apple cheeks finally dimpled with a smile, and knew he couldn't deny her.

"Okay, olives," he said, handing her the can, which she hugged to her. "And what'll we have with them?"

"Ummmm..." She studied her options again and spotted a box displayed on the top shelf. "Cookies!" She pointed again.

She was a woman after his own heart. Olives and brownies were among his favorites, though he couldn't recall having had them together.

He took the box of fancy cookies down and placed it on the counter. "Okay. Cookies for dessert. But we need something else. Let's try the freezer."

He put her down to protect her from the blast of cold air and stared in surprise at the stacks of marked freezer bags. "Whoa," he said to Savannah. "Your uncle Darren's been here."

"Who's that?" she asked, still hugging her olives.

"My brother," he said, pulling out several packages. "He owns a restaurant, so we get lots of good stuff to eat."

"I have a brother. Zachary."

"Right. Maybe you'll get lucky, too, and someday he'll keep you in food. Let's see what we've got. Veal Marsala, beef bourgignon, shrimp creole, chicken strips—"

"Yeah!" she shouted, the smile growing even wider. He felt drunk with success.

"All right. Chicken strips, it is."

He opened the can and Savannah stood on the step stool and poured the olives into a bowl while he followed Darren's microwave directions for the chicken strips.

Jared gained hope for their curious alliance during lunch. Savannah, obviously feeling more comfortable, ate well and told him she liked the "big window in the room with all the blue in it."

"The window seat," Libby interpreted, the baby asleep in his carrier in the chair beside her.

"There's a window seat in your room, too," he told Savannah, mentally reassigning rooms. He'd thought to put her in the smaller room that adjoined his and give Libby the big room opposite. But the big room had the window seat.

"Is it pink?" Savannah asked.

It wasn't. When he'd repainted the upstairs last year, he'd intended to use that room for an office, but had been too busy to move things over from the workshop. The room had a wall of built-in storage, but he guessed it would serve even better for toys than it would have paperwork.

"No, it's white," he replied.

She looked accusatory. "I like pink."

"Then we'll paint it." He was learning to deal with her. Parenthood wasn't so hard. All you had to do was everything the child wanted.

Libby appeared to disapprove.

He toasted her with the last sip in his coffee cup. "You nanny your way—I'll parent mine."

She shook her head at him. "And you'll be in a straitjacket afore me," she said, taking a few liberties with the high-road, low-road ditty. "But I know—" she forestalled him when he would have spoken "—it isn't my concern. I just give you fair warning if you proceed this way, you'll need the marines to maintain order before she's twelve."

"What are you?" he asked. "Twenty-one? Twenty-two?"

She was blushing with the enormity of the compliment, until she remembered she wasn't thirty-five now, but twenty-five. And that's what she told him.

"And how long have you been in the nanny business?"

She had to analyze her answer a moment. "Not that long," she finally replied.

"Then where does all this knowledge about children come from?" The question suggested that she might think she knew more than she did.

"I have a degree in education," she said, angling her chin a little huffily. "I illustrate children's books."

He pushed his coffee cup away and rested an elbow on the back of his chair, studying her with new interest. "You do? Then why are you here?"

She made a production of straightening Zachary's blanket, though he hadn't stirred, taking the time to remind herself sharply to be careful. Landing this job wasn't a direct path to getting the children. She had to *keep* it until her employer fell apart under the strain. So she had to maintain her story.

She smiled. Her cheeks were red. He had a way of studying her that made her feel he was simply humoring her, that he was onto her performance. But that was impossible. So she tried to pass off the blush as embarrassment.

"That is, I *want* to be an illustrator of children's books. I have a manuscript at a publisher's right now. It's all very real in my mind. It just hasn't happened yet. And I have to support myself until it does."

He eyed her with that look that always made her feel she was a hairbreadth from discovery. "You mean a publisher could offer you a contract at any moment and take you away from us?"

Take you away from us. Us. He sounded very much as though he already considered the children and him a unit. She resented that. But she couldn't afford to let him think her wishes for the children weren't the same as his.

"I'm sure I'd have to produce several books before I could hope to support myself from the income," she assured him quickly. "And by then you'll probably be so good at parenting, you won't even need a nanny any longer."

He smiled dryly. "Right. But until then, we have your complete attention?"

"Of course."

"Good."

J ARED WAS RELIEVED that Savannah seemed to like her bedroom. From Portland he'd called Justine Potter, who managed his ARCHI-JUNK outlet, and asked her to have the white wrought-iron daybeds moved in from the shop. He saw that she'd covered this one, which he'd originally intended as Libby's, with a wedding-ring quilt and thrown half a dozen decorative pillows on it.

Savannah ran a hand over the bed, then went straight to the window seat and climbed onto it to peer out. There were pine trees to look at, and a whitecapped ocean rolling out into a foggy horizon. A blurred sun peered out, raying spectacular bars of light in all directions. A small *faux* porch only about a foot wide but with the same decorative fretwork used in the front, ran the length of the window.

The child put her hands against the small panes of glass, studied the dramatic view and asked gravely, "Is that where heaven is?"

Libby, standing back with the baby carrier at her feet, opened her mouth as though to reply, then seemed to change her mind. Apparently she remembered that just yesterday he'd insisted that he wasn't expecting her to assume his obligations, but simply to support him. And certainly trying to explain heaven was a parental obligation. The kind that made one want to run the other way.

He went to stand behind Savannah and look out at what she saw. "Heaven is wherever God is," he said, thinking even as the words were spoken that they sounded like hedging.

She pointed to the broad bands of light. "Is that Him?"

He sorted through his mind for old Sunday-school lessons, for things he hadn't thought about in years.

"Yes," he replied. "He's in the sky and in the ocean, and the trees and the birds and the earth. He's everywhere. He takes care of everything."

She turned away from the window to look at him with probing eyes. "How do you know?"

"Because He made everything. And He watches over it."

"Libby says Mommy and Daddy are with Him."

"That's right."

She put a little hand on his shoulder and raised her foot to pull up her sock. "What do you think they're doing now?"

He wasn't sure how long he could continue to think in her terms. "Well . . . probably the same thing you're doing. They probably just had lunch, and maybe they're going to put their things away and take a walk."

She frowned at him. "I don't think so."

Oh-oh. "Why not?" he asked, thinking he'd erred in some major way.

She put both hands on his shoulders and told him patiently, "People in heaven fly. They have wings."

"I see." He swung her down to the carpet.

Libby was looking at him as though he'd done something seriously wrong. He knew his theology was shaky, but then, sharing it with children certainly should allow for variations.

Savannah ran to the bed and threw herself into the nest of pillows.

"What?" Jared asked Libby. "How would you have explained?"

"You explained beautifully," she said in a cool tone that seemed to suggest the opposite. "I couldn't have done any better."

"Then why are you glaring at me?"

"I'm not glaring," she denied, even as she continued to do so.

She made a production of putting one of Savannah's suitcases on the bed. He suspected it was simply so she didn't have to look at him.

"Libby," he said quietly. "We're going to have to work together."

She glanced up at him then, blue eyes distressed but still cool. "I thought we had a definite division of duties. You're the parent—I'm just the nanny."

"You're not *just* the nanny," he heard himself retort, amazed that this quietly quarrelsome conversation was taking place. Where had it come from? Where the hell was it going? And why was he engaged in it, he who never succumbed to a woman's manipulative behavior? "I know you're important to the children."

He watched in amazement as tears formed in her eyes. She looked about to burst with some hot retort, but she finally just drew a deep breath. Her small bosom swelled several inches, completely distracting him, then she tossed her head and brushed the tears away. She suddenly seemed very quiet.

"If you'll show me my room now," she suggested, "maybe Savannah and I can both take a nap. I didn't sleep very well last night and Savannah's had a long morning."

"Right." He led her across the hall to the small green-and-cream room that adjoined his. It, too, contained a white wrought-iron daybed, only this one had a coverlet patterned with zoo animals and clowns.

He explained when Libby raised a questioning eyebrow. "It'll be simple enough to change the bedspreads," he said.

She opened the wide wardrobe doors and said ironically, "I can fill only about six inches of that." Then she went to the other door and opened it.

She glanced at the beige-and-brown room Justine had tidied to make it almost unrecognizable as his, then closed the door and asked calmly, "Yours?"

"Yes."

"You're very neat."

"The young woman who runs my shop comes in a few hours a week to try to keep me that way. She's a friend of the family." He glanced around Libby's room. "As I said, I'd intended this room for Savannah, but she has a thing for window seats. You can lock it from this side if you'd feel more comfortable."

She sat on the bed and bounced a little. "I don't think that will be necessary. His lordship seducing the nanny is an archaic practice, isn't it?"

He leaned a shoulder in the open doorway and folded his arms. "Probably depends on the seductive qualities of the nanny."

She stopped bouncing and looked up at him, blue eyes startled. "Or the lasciviousness of the lord."

"Takes two to minuet." And that was as far as he was going with that. He had no idea why he'd started it anyway, except that she behaved like such a little know-it-all—except for that brief and curious interlude a few moments ago when she'd seemed more like a little lost-it-all. He wanted her to remember that some things couldn't be predicted.

In fact, he thought he'd be wise to remember it himself.

He turned to leave. "I'll bring your bags up," he called over his shoulder, "and you girls can nap."

Chapter Three

Libby rounded the corner into the kitchen, a just-awakened Zachary in her arms, and muttered a little gasp of alarm when she almost collided with ... it took her a moment to identify the object. A cradle? It was being carried on its side, so she found it difficult to tell. It was made of wicker and appeared antique.

Then she noticed the woman carrying it. She was average in height, and wore jeans and a Seattle Mariners sweatshirt. Shoulder-length dark hair was tied back in a ponytail, revealing a pretty, heart-shaped face.

Dark-brown eyes smiled warmly as she put the cradle down and offered her hand. "Hi!" she said. "I'm Justine—Justy—Potter. I work for Jared. I'm sorry I frightened you. You're the nanny?"

Libby held the baby to her with her left arm and shook hands. "Yes. Elizabeth Madison. But everyone calls me 'Libby.' And this is Zachary." She turned him so that Justine could see him.

"Well, aren't *you* just the cutest thing." She took Zachary from her while launching into a long string of baby-talk words.

Zachary watched her with wide blue eyes, his plump arms moving excitedly as she carried on.

"Well, I was dusting off this cradle in the shop today and thought it was just made for you," she crooned as she placed the baby in it.

He launched into loud screams.

"Well," she said with a frown, pulling him out again. "Maybe not."

"No, it's wonderful," Libby said, picking it up and carrying it toward the table as Justine followed, bouncing the squalling baby. "He just got up from a nap. I think he doesn't want to lie down again until he's sure he's going to get something to eat."

She took a bottle from the refrigerator, ran it under hot water, then pointed to the cradle. "Now put him in it." She sat in the chair near the cradle and leaned down to support the bottle, while Justine sat on the other side and gently rocked.

Zachary ate noisily, little hands waving his delight with the arrangements.

"Isn't there another child?" Justine asked.

"Savannah. She's four, and in the middle of a nap."

"Quite a life-style change for Jared." Justine straightened, crossed her legs and pushed on the cradle with the toe of her suede boot. "Have you met the rest of the family?"

"No, but I've eaten Darren's chicken strips. I understand he has a restaurant."

Justine heaved a sigh and grimaced. "On the bay side of the peninsula. Very posh, trendy spot. I used to work for him. He's a pain in the posterior. Their mother's a total nut, but very wonderful."

"Mr. Ransom," Libby said, probing carefully, "is pretty remarkable to take in two children."

Justy played with the baby's fingers and gave Libby a significant glance. "Well, they are *Mandy's* children, after all."

"Yes. They were good friends, weren't they?"

Justy straightened, her smile thinning. "They were going to be married until she met Frank. Maybe people can't help whom they fall in love with." She uttered a small, rueful laugh that seemed suddenly very personal. Then she shook her head and refocused on Libby. "At least that's how Jared chose to look at it—but he really loved Mandy. I think for her, loving Frank was less demanding than loving Jared."

"So you knew her?"

"Not very well. I was seeing a lot of Darren at the time, and we went to Connecticut to visit Jared for his birthday. Frank had come to spend time with Jared between jobs and . . ." She indicated the baby. "Well, the rest of the story is now living under this roof. And quite beautiful." She leaned over Zachary and smoothed his pink cheek. "They'll be happy here."

Libby didn't want to hear that. She wanted to know the children would be happy, of course, but she wanted them to be happy with *her.* The selfishness of that thought troubled her.

Justy straightened abruptly. "Well. What would you like for dinner? I usually get it started."

"Oh . . . I'm sure Jared should make that decision." Libby was having difficulty following from subject to subject.

The back door opened and Jared walked in carrying what appeared to be a large, flat table. Until he kicked the door closed and walked across the kitchen and she saw that it was a folded drafting table.

"Can you use this?" he asked Libby, easing it to the floor and balancing it there with one hand.

She looked from him to it in amazement. She'd left hers at home, not sure there'd be room here to set one up.

"Ah...yes. Of course. I'd love it."

"Good. I picked it up at an estate sale months ago and held on to it, thinking I'd use it sometime, but it's just sat around in the back of the workshop." His eyes fell on Zachary, his bottle being held by one woman while his cradle was rocked by another, and he grinned. "He looks starved for attention. Good use for that cradle. Way to go, Zach. Get your women working for you."

Justine gave Zachary's toes a gentle pinch and stood. "I could have a baby just like him, if Darren wasn't so selfish."

Jared shook his head at Justy, obviously exasperated. "Darren isn't selfish. He just doesn't believe in distributing children around the countryside without benefit of marriage to their mother."

"I explained that." Justine folded her arms. "We'd be a family. Just not a married one."

"That's crazy."

"It's contemporary. And the sanest solution for a woman who doesn't believe in marriage but wants children."

Jared shook his head and picked up the table again. "You're nuts, Potter. I've said it before and I'll say it again. You need a shrink."

Justine fixed him with a look that was both affectionate and frustrated. "And you need to stop thinking like an antiquarian and come into the new millenium. What do you want for dinner?"

He turned to Libby and she met his gaze with amusement in her eyes. She was fascinated that the issue of making babies could be discussed in the same breath as what to have for dinner.

"Do you have a preference?" he asked.

She shook her head. "Your choice. Savannah had a big lunch, so I doubt she'll do more than just pick."

"Chicken and noodles?" Justine suggested. "Kids usually like noodles."

"All right," Jared said approvingly. "Libby, can you come up with me for a minute and tell me where you want this?"

"Of course." She began to scoop up the baby, but Justine shooed her away. "I'll watch him. Take your time."

Libby followed Jared up the narrow back stairs, then he stood aside to let her precede him into her room. She went to the window where a small wicker chair sat and moved it aside to make room.

"Right here," she said.

He unfolded the legs and set the table down. "Facing the window, or turned to the side to get the light from it?"

"Turned," she said, picking up one side to give him help he didn't need in moving it. "This is north light. It'll be perfect."

She felt a stirring of excitement at the touch of the laminated board under her hands. Illustration wasn't her priority right now, but the need to make art was in her blood and wouldn't be denied for long. She knew she'd be able to work it smoothly into her life with the children once they were hers.

"What else do you need?" he asked, frowning over the table looking rather naked in the gray light of late afternoon.

"Grounding!" she thought desperately, experiencing a strange and sudden disconnection from her surroundings.

It was all so immediate—the touch of the board under her fingertips, the bright intelligence and interest in Jared's dark eyes.

But this was her past—or a second chance at her past—with everything she'd ever wanted in it.

Did that really ever happen to anyone? She couldn't believe that it did, but it was happening to her!

"You'll need a place to put your paints and materials. What do you call those things with drawers?" Jared's hand sketched a low table in the air at about his knee level.

She put all her disorienting thoughts aside to answer him.

"A tabaret," she said.

"Right. And you'll need somewhere to put yourself when you're using it. A stool, maybe? I think we have an old bar stool with a back in the shop."

"Please," she told him. "You aren't required to provide what I need for my spare-time activities." She didn't want him to think her art would interfere with her obligations to the children. Particularly since she ultimately intended to win them from him. Determination and guilt, she decided as she shifted her weight uncomfortably, were quarrelsome emotions when carried together.

"You have to have something to do with your weekends," he said politely. He managed to reinforce, she thought with a sigh, the point that she was employed, and would be expected to stay out of their way when she was off duty.

It occurred to her for the first time that weekends would probably be awkward. Would she have to leave the house? Provide her own food? She had no cooking facilities.

She couldn't very well take a motel room for two days.

"The bar stool would be great, thank you," she said, unconsciously adjusting the table to the angle she preferred. "And I can get by without a tabaret and make do with a flat table." She looked around her for something she could cover with a cloth, but a small escritoire, and a little table by the chair she'd moved both looked too valuable to put to such use.

"I'm sure I've got something in the workshop I can bring over," he said. "Anything else you need?"

"I do have a question about weekends."

He rested his hands on his hips. "What is it?"

"Would you like me . . . out of the house?"

He seemed to be trying to measure the question—and possibly her mood after their little exchange when they'd parted company earlier in the day.

"You mean because you're just the nanny?" he asked. His expression was straight, but she saw the humor in his eyes.

She had to get on a comfortable footing here, so she swallowed her pride. "All right. I apologize. But I've never been..." She stopped herself just in time. She had to remain alert! "I've never been a live-in nanny before. I'm not sure about the protocol."

He nodded and folded his arms, obviously taking her seriously. "Fair enough. I've never employed one before, so we'll probably both be learning as we go. Right now, as far as I'm concerned, you can leave if you like, but you aren't required to. Where would you eat and sleep?"

She felt great relief. "I don't know. That was my question."

"Look. You live here. But weekends will be yours. You can work up here, or you can come downstairs and entertain yourself however you like. Town's an easy mile walk, and Justy's always running off to Longview to shop—that's about an hour away—or to Astoria. There are a few things to see there, several nice galleries. Do whatever you like. On Saturdays and Sundays, you can come and go. The difference will be that if you're home and the children call or cry, you don't have to respond."

How could she *not?* She'd have to try to cooperate. She didn't want to alienate him and have him fire her before she got the children from him.

Plus the salary he paid her and the conditions he offered were more than generous. She was grateful for that. Had the situation been different, she might have found him appealing.

Well. Truth to tell, she did find him appealing. But if the situation were different, she'd do something about it.

"All right," she said. "Thank you."

"Sure. Anything else?"

The sound of a child crying suddenly penetrated the upstairs quiet. Libby ran across the hall, Jared right behind her, and found Savannah standing in the middle of the room looking sleepy and disheveled, wringing her little hands.

Libby dropped to one knee in front of her and took hold of her arms. "What, sweetie? I'm right here."

"I forgot where the bathroom is." She wept urgently.

Libby pointed to the door at the end of the room. "Right there, Savannah. You have your own. Do you want me to—"

"No. I can do it by myself." And Savannah ran.

Libby pushed herself to her feet, relieved that the crisis had been so ordinary. She turned to find Jared standing just inside the door, watching her with a thin, reluctant smile.

Then she realized what she'd done.

"Am I not supposed to respond if you're around?" she asked. This was going to be so much more difficult than she'd imagined.

He shook his head at her, the gesture almost indulgent. "I think you'd implode if I asked you to do that. You're sure you haven't been at this very long? You seem to have well-honed child-care instincts."

She made a careless gesture with one hand. "I'm a woman."

His glance swept her from head to foot with an acceptance of that declaration that managed to be respectful and unnerving at the same time.

"That you are," he said. Then he turned away from her to look around the room. "So, what do you think? Should we paint this pink?"

Perfectly willing to let the matter drop, she began a serious study of her surroundings. "Actually, I was thinking that I could paint a border on it for Savannah, if you don't mind. And if we can get her to agree. It would create much less disturbance. You wouldn't have to move everything out or cover it."

"What would you paint?"

Savannah reappeared, her cheeks flushed from sleep but her eyes now wide and bright. Her rich brown braids were in disarray.

Libby pointed to the wall of cupboards and drawers. "Shall we paint Rosie on your wall, Savannah? And make some kitty pillows for your window seat?"

Savannah looked up at the wall they studied. "Pink ones?" she asked.

"Sure. Maybe some in every color."

"Who's Rosie?" Jared asked.

"Rosie Posie," Savannah said, moving to his side, her eyes wide. "She flies. She gots wings."

"Ah." He lifted her up into his arms. "An angel."

"No. A little girl. Like me. Libby made her."

Jared looked beyond the child to Libby for an explanation.

"She's in the book I'm trying to sell," she explained. "Her mom's an executive, and the nanny has Rosie's twin baby brothers to claim her attention, so Rosie Posie and her cat sprout wings and go off on adventures."

He smiled. "Obviously a less vigilant nanny than you are."

"Obviously."

"Do you have everything you need for the project?"

"I'll look my paints over. I might need a few colors. But I'll draw it up first and get Savannah's and your approval."

"All right with you?" he asked Savannah. "Libby's going to make a picture of what she's going to paint."

"Yeah," she said. "I want to paint, too."

Jared looked doubtfully at Libby.

"Sure," she said. "We'll give her one drawer, or one closet door she can do herself. Wouldn't that be all right?"

"It's your masterpiece."

A squeal from the baby downstairs made Libby turn in that direction. Then she turned back, not sure whether Jared wanted to be left with Savannah.

"Go to Justine's rescue," he said. "We'll be fine."

She hurried off, thinking that things just might be taking a positive turn. He seemed to be willing to work with her if she showed a cooperative frame of mind.

That was good. It might help to make a friend of him before she tried to convince him she'd make the better parent.

"WHAT'S IN THERE?" Savannah asked, pointing to the drawers and closets under discussion.

"Nothing right now," Jared said, taking a few steps forward and opening a closet door so that she could peer inside. "But when your toys come, we'll put them all in here."

"But they're home."

"I had a big truck pick them up at home, and now they're on their way to you."

She smiled, seeming to like that idea. "I gots a Katie Cooking Kitchen." She spread her arms, seemingly to indicate that it was enormous. "An' a beauty shop."

"Wow."

She put small fingers to the hair on his forehead. "I can curl your hair."

"Oh, boy," he said. Life as a parent would take some adjustment, but he was willing to bet it would be the small things that made the biggest impact on him.

For instance, when he'd decided to do this, he'd had no idea there'd be such pleasure in simply holding a child, in feeling her warmth as she leaned trustingly against him. He'd had no idea how eagerly he'd wait for a smile, or how it would warm him when it came and make him think that maybe *this* was what it was all about, rather than any other kind of success.

Savannah looked into his eyes and he saw Frank there—serious, earnest, but with a spark of humor tucked away. Then she smiled and he saw Mandy— charming, flirtatious, greedy for life.

He'd resolved the anger that had ruled him for months after they'd told him they were in love. He'd moved to another project, and felt mature and magnanimous when he'd sent a wedding gift in response to their invitation. But he hadn't gone to the wedding.

Then Frank had called and begged him to come back for their baby's baptism. When he'd pleaded overwork, Mandy had gotten on the phone and told him they'd talked it over and decided that even if he couldn't forgive them, they wanted to know that their child would always belong in some part to him.

And he hadn't known how to dismiss that trust.

And as Savannah now wrapped her arms around his neck, he was glad he hadn't.

"I like you," she said, as though sure he'd been waiting to hear that.

He had.

LIBBY SMILED at the freshly bathed child in her Pocahontas pajamas. She'd eaten a reasonable portion of chicken and noodles, helped Libby load the dishwasher and clean up the kitchen, and had been bribed into going to bed with promises of a Rosie story.

Savannah crawled under the covers and snuggled in, her balding gingerbread man in the crook of her arm. "The one about her at that place with the tall thing."

"The Eiffel Tower." Libby sat on the edge of the bed and turned the beside lamp onto its lowest setting. Rosie in Paris was her favorite, too.

Slowly, quietly, she spun out the story of the little six-year-old who made friends with a stray tuxedo cat and discovered that when she held the cat and wished very hard, her dreams came true.

And because she'd been supplanted in everyone's attention by two screaming baby brothers, her dream was always to go far away and visit the places where her mother went on business.

When her mother went to Paris to close an important deal, Rosie and Tuxedo followed after her.

They flew over the Eiffel Tower, the Arc de triomphe, Notre Dame and all the other attractions that drew tourists. When they tired of that, they ate *croissants* at a *boulangerie,* drank tea in a sidewalk *café,* and went shopping on the Champs-Élysées.

Savannah's favorite part was when they stowed away on a barge on the Seine and were discovered by the captain, but instead of calling the police, the captain shared his *pâté* and crackers with them.

At the end of the book, Rosie and Tux bump into her mother at Tour d'Argent and they all flew home together on the Concorde. But Libby left out that part, afraid of reminding Savannah that her own mother could not be found.

"So, where does she go after that?" Savannah wanted to know.

"I think to Rome," Libby replied. "She wants to see the pigeons at the Vatican. But we'll save that story for tomorrow night, okay?"

"Okay."

Libby leaned over to kiss her cheek, then stood to turn out the light, and noticed Jared in the doorway, a shoulder leaning against the molding, a very wide-awake Zachary in his arms.

He straightened and walked into the room. "Good story," he praised as they passed each other at the foot of the bed. "But when you and Rosie go to Rome tomorrow night, the pigeons are at Saint Peter's, not the Vatican."

Libby hated being wrong. It had been a lifelong frailty. But she smiled in the shadows and said softly, "Pigeons are generally everywhere. I don't think Savannah cares about that."

He tipped his head in a "probably so" gesture. "I just thought if you send that story off to a publisher, *you* might care. Would you hold Zack while I say goodnight to Savannah?"

"Of course," she answered stiffly, and left the room in a slight huff. But she lingered outside to listen. She had every right, she told herself. She was going to be Savannah's mother.

"Everything okay?" she heard Jared ask. "You comfortable?"

"Yeah," the child replied in a small voice. "Tomorrow can I paint?"

"Sure."

"Can I have those noodles again?"

"You liked those?"

He sounded pleased. Something in his voice prodded her sense of righteousness and bled a little drop of guilt. She tossed her head and ignored it.

"They were yummy."

"I liked them, too. We'll have the leftovers tomorrow."

"Okay."

She sounded sleepy. The bedcovers rustled. Libby imagined that Jared leaned over to kiss her good-night.

He confirmed that an instant later with a throaty "Good night, Savannah."

"'Night . . . I forgot your name."

"Jared."

"'Night, Jared."

"'Night, baby."

Libby dashed toward the stairs when she heard Jared get to his feet. She ran lightly down them, through the kitchen and into the living room, where she sat on the sofa with the baby, trying very much to look as though she'd been there since she'd left him.

She propped Zachary up against the corner pillows and made faces at him. He studied her gravely.

When Jared appeared, she glanced up at him, innocence in her eyes. "Everything okay?"

"Seems to be," he replied, picking the baby up and sitting in his place, then holding him before him and letting Zachary's toes rest on his thighs.

Nice thighs, she noticed absently, long and athletic, rather than bunched and bulbous.

"But then, you know that, don't you?" he asked conversationally, not even turning to look at her. "You heard everything I said to Savannah."

She gasped indignantly, but he sent her a scolding glance that cut it short.

"Don't play with me, Libby," he said, lifting the baby high so that the infant smiled widely and shrieked. "I thought we had this out last night. I admitted I had a lot to learn. Why do you feel you have to spy on me?"

"I wasn't spying on you," she denied, moving aside to put a little more distance between them.

"You were watching me, thinking that I couldn't see you." He smiled at the delighted baby as he hoisted him for another bounce. "What do you call that?"

She thought fast. "I . . . I was standing by . . . in case I was needed."

"Good try," he said, sitting Zachary on his knees and bouncing him. "I think the truth is, you don't trust me . . . yet you admitted you aren't that much more experienced at dealing with children than I am."

She opened her mouth to rebut. He interrupted her before she could begin. "And don't give me that stuff about your being a woman. We're supposed to be an enlightened generation. We know that men can nurture just as well as women."

"I was just . . . trying to be conscientious."

"You were spying. And if I find you doing that again, I'll let you go."

Panic seized her. She fought to keep her head. "If you're serious about being a good father," she said calmly, "you'll have to learn to be less judgmental and listen to the other side of the story before you start making threats."

"I will never," he said quietly, very seriously, "be the kind of father—or the kind of employer—who counts to three. I will get cooperation when I ask for it, or consequences happen."

She'd always considered counting a self-defeating style of discipline, but she was in no mood to agree with him. And she was hardly in a position to disagree. She looked for neutral ground.

"I guess," she said, trying to appear penitent without seeming cowed, "I was a little worried that the pain the children's parents must have caused you would affect..."

She closed her eyes for a moment over her own ignorance. She certainly had a lot to learn about subterfuge.

"Justy told me," she admitted before he could ask how she knew what Mandy had been to him. "It wasn't deliberate. We were discussing the children and it just sort of... came out."

He looked as though he wasn't sure what to be most angry about—the fact that she and Justy had been discussing him, or that she'd questioned his motives in taking the children.

His eyes darkened as he tucked the baby into the crook of his arm so that he could give Libby his full attention.

"You thought I'd take out my disappointments on two helpless children?"

Spoken aloud, it was a reprehensible question. But if he wanted frankness, she'd give it to him—as much as she dared.

"I didn't know," she replied, looking him in the eye. "But I spent several days with the children while they were in the hospital, and grew very attached to them. I...I was very pleased when you...when the agency sent me to you because that meant I could...keep an eye on them. They came to mean a lot to me."

He held her defensive stare, and she saw a very subtle softening in his eyes. But it did not reflect itself in his jaw—or his manner.

"I'm glad to know that," he said finally, "but I'm beginning to think we've made a mistake here. I do want a nanny who cares, but you don't seem to be able to remember that these children are mine and not yours. And that my life is none of your business."

Inside she bristled, but struggled frantically to regain lost ground.

"I thought you'd want me to think of them as mine," she said, sounding miffed. It was half pretense, half truth. "I don't think halfhearted care would be good for any child. Particularly two who've just suffered a great loss."

"I think a good nanny," he said, running a knuckle down the baby's cheek when he fretted, apparently reacting to the tones of their voices, "would be able to accomplish that without getting in my way—or spying on me."

"The service provides a week's trial period," she lied—convincingly, she thought. "If you're unhappy with me, the agency will pay my wages and you won't have to."

He frowned. "Mrs. Grover told me I could call for a replacement at any time if I was unhappy," he said.

Oh, boy. "Well . . . Mrs. Grover's our substitute supervisor. Mrs. Baldwin's had knee-replacement surgery. An old ice-skating injury." She smiled amiably. "Competed for Canada in the Olympics in her youth." He didn't react. "Ice dancing, I believe. Doubles." His expression remained reproachful. "Grover's a career nanny. Spent most of her time in private care before she came to . . . to us."

Her fabrication was becoming more and more lame, and she wanted to get off the subject before he began to ask for details she wouldn't be able to supply.

"Anyway, you have me until next Wednesday, free of charge." She knew good form—and the success of her mission here—required that she apologize. "I will do my best to try not to interfere with your role as—" it was so hard for her to say it "—parent...if you bear in mind that my role is awkward, and try not to be so sensitive."

He looked at her as though he were no longer entirely sure who or what he was dealing with. "I'm sorry," he said, his tone still defensive, "but when I'm spied on, or when I'm suspected of harboring abusive tendencies, I tend to get sensitive."

The baby began to howl.

Libby held her hand out to take him. "Want me to try to quiet him down?"

Jared ignored her and stood, turning the baby onto his stomach as she'd done the day before. "No, thanks," he said. "As of seven, you're off the clock. The rest of the evening's yours. Good night." And he headed for the kitchen.

Libby went to her room, closed the door and leaned against it with a groan of exasperation. It wasn't hard to conclude that she was becoming her own worst enemy here. She had to calm down, settle down, *pipe* down.

She was not behaving like a nanny at all, but like a woman who was stark, raving mad. If she didn't pull it together, he was going to figure out that she was serving her own agenda and not his, and then he would figure out why. And she could kiss the children goodbye—literally.

And she hadn't retraced ten years in time to let that happen.

Tomorrow, she resolved, dropping her clothes around her in a puddle in her private bath, she would be the epitome of decorum and cooperation.

She stepped under the hot shower, vowing that she would not question him under any circumstances, and she would definitely never eavesdrop on him again. He was bound to tire of the novelty of parenthood eventually, then she would have the children mostly to herself. At that point, she could employ her own strategies to get them away from him.

JARED LAY on the carpet in front of the fireplace with Zachary and laughed when he laughed as they played a game of peekaboo with a blanket.

This was good, he thought. They were building a rapport. The only problem was it was after midnight and this baby showed no sign of slowing down.

Savannah, at least, was sleeping soundly. He'd gone upstairs several times to check on her.

And things were quiet from the nanny's room. He wondered what her game was. He was smart enough to be sure she had one.

Maybe her overzealousness came from a desire to make a name for herself. Maybe she had big dreams of serving as a nanny to a political family, or an entertainment one. Wasn't that how many young women met wealthy, powerful husbands?

But how would that fit in with her career as an illustrator? Unless finding a wealthy, powerful husband would allow her to devote full time to her art. She'd said it would be years before the art could support itself.

The baby yawned and rubbed his eyes, and Jared scooped him up and sat with him in the rocker before he could perk up again. He wrapped the blanket around him and patted his back in the way he'd seen Libby do.

Libby. The woman was a mystery, all right; but he allowed no mysteries in his life. He prided himself on being able to trace the history and origin of everything he found in his architectural salvage explorations. And he would figure her out, too.

She was obviously skilled with children, though she'd admitted to a short time in the nanny service. That truth was borne out more by her inability to be unobtrusive in her work, than in the work itself.

He guessed her skill resulted from the research she did for her work, and what appeared to be a natural affinity for entering a child's mysterious places and being able to function there.

That was what terrified him most. The fear that he wouldn't be able to find his way into the children's confidence because he couldn't remember what it was like to think like a child.

Life as an adult was so complex. And his relationship with their parents had been so complicated even *he* hadn't understood it. All he'd known was that—and this had astounded him—the pain they'd caused him had not erased the love he felt for them.

Zachary finally asleep in his arms, Jared got carefully out of the chair, turned off the lights and headed upstairs. He was too tired to try to untangle philosophical mysteries tonight.

He put the baby in the crib in Savannah's room and breathed a sigh of relief when he didn't wake up.

Savannah's covers were down to her waist and he pulled them up, tucked them in, then drew the door half-closed behind him as he left.

He went quietly across the hall, shed his clothes and climbed into bed, thinking he hadn't been this tired since boot camp.

He glanced at the door that connected his room to Libby's, then turned deliberately away from it. He needed peaceful dreams tonight.

Chapter Four

"When's *he* gonna get up?" Savannah asked, following Libby around the kitchen as she warmed a bottle for Zachary and looked for something to take the edge off the little girl's hunger while she fed the baby.

Libby glanced out the window at the incredible view of a long stretch of sand merging with gentle breakers under a lightening sky. "Probably pretty soon. Zachary kept him up for a long time last night."

She'd heard the faint sounds of his laughter into the night, and halfway hoped he'd come to knock on her door and plead for her help in getting the baby to sleep.

But he hadn't. Then she'd finally heard him come upstairs, heard him detour into the children's room before going into his. Then the house had been silent.

She'd told herself comfortingly that anyone could be patient one time. But when he was awakened night after night, certainly his patience would wane.

So she'd gotten up this morning, determined to be the quintessential nanny. He would find no fault with her if she could help it.

But she wouldn't mind looking a little smug and superior when he awoke to find that she'd already fed the children and gotten a start on the day.

She put Zachary's cereal in the microwave, then took a banana from a fruit bowl on the edge of the counter and gave half of it to Savannah.

Adding cold milk to the cereal to cool it, she turned on cartoons on the small kitchen television and sat in one of the kitchen chairs to feed Zachary.

He was nearly finished, when she heard the sudden sound of dogs barking outside. Before she could get up to investigate, she heard a key in the lock and saw the knob turn. She gasped, uncertain whether or not to be alarmed, then the door opened. She was assailed instantly by what appeared to be the total occupancy of the local pound.

A small black-and-white dog she guessed to be a terrier ran at her, claws clicking on the kitchen tile. The last two inches of his black tail were white and traveled behind him like a battle flag. He trailed a red fabric leash attached to his red collar.

He put his forelegs on her knee, sniffed her and the baby, then turned to Savannah's delighted squeals.

A smaller and very hairy white dog came at her, yipping wildly. He barked several times, whether in warning, disapproval or greeting she wasn't certain. Then he followed the black-and-white dog to Savannah.

A big golden retriever with a slow gait and a gray muzzle that betrayed age wandered in, long, plumy tail swishing as it spotted her and came to investigate.

Libby was wondering which dog had unlocked the door, when a tall man dressed in a tuxedo walked in, carrying two bags of groceries.

Okay. Dogs and men in tuxedos at seven o'clock in the morning. She could handle going back in time, but she'd be darned if she'd allow the past to go Salvador Dali on her. She began to stand up.

Then the man turned to her and she saw that he was blond, probably in his late twenties or early thirties, and smiling apologetically in her direction.

"No, don't let us disturb you," he said as he dropped the bags on the counter. "You're the nanny? Lizzie?"

"Libby," she corrected.

"Glad to meet you. Hope we didn't alarm you. I often come over uninvited—mostly because I never *get* invited. I'm Darren Ransom, Jared's brother."

Of course. She smiled as he came to look down on the baby. "The chicken strips," she said, then remembered what Justine had said about him and decided she could certainly see why she'd wanted him to father her children. He was as tall as Jared, but more slender, more elegantly featured. He would have fathered beautiful offspring.

He nodded as he caught the baby's flailing hand between his thumb and forefinger and grinned at him. "I often bring Jared leftovers, but I thought he'd need stuff off the children's menu, too, this time. Where is he?"

"The baby kept him up late," she replied. "I think he's still sleeping."

Darren shook his head. "God. I can't believe he's doing this." He straightened and turned at the sound of hilarious giggles. Savannah had the little white dog in her lap and was being thoroughly kissed. He smiled indulgently. "Georgia?" he asked.

She laughed lightly. "Close. Savannah."

He shook his head again. "Two of them. I can't believe it. Of course, I'm sure hiring you will make it possible for him to cope."

She returned his kind smile, thinking that she soon hoped to make it unnecessary for Jared even to try.

"I'll do my best."

"Fine. Leave your old mother to carry ten pounds of apples, twenty pounds of potatoes and the world's largest pumpkin." That complaint was accompanied into the room by a short, rotund woman in a bright-red coat and matching short-brimmed hat.

Her hair was very white and blunt-cut to just below her ears, with the very contemporary shaved nape visible under the hat. On her feet were attractive but serviceable wedge-heeled shoes.

Darren turned quickly to remove the bag of apples she carried in one arm. He placed it on the counter, then took the sack of potatoes she dragged with the other hand.

"What did you do with the pumpkin?" he asked.

She jerked a thumb behind her, presumably in the direction of the car in which they'd come. "It was big enough to turn into a coach. I figured it could get into the house on its own."

Darren cast Libby a rolling-eyed glance at the joke. "Libby, this is Jared and my mother, Carlotta Ransom. Mom, this is Libby, the nanny. In her arms is Zachary. And that's Savannah, being ravaged by your brat pack."

Savannah was now on the floor, giggles turning to shrieks of laughter as the little dogs pinned her with kisses. Even the retriever ambled over to investigate, her tail swishing.

The woman went toward the little girl, a hand pressed over her heart as though she couldn't quite believe what she was seeing. A small smile formed on her lips. Her face glowed as if from some deep satisfaction.

"Grandchildren," she murmured. "At last. Savannah?"

Loud yipping and her own giggles prevented Savannah from hearing her.

"Spike! Tippy!" Carlotta said firmly. "Stop terrorizing that child! Scarlett, come to Mama."

Spike and Tippy didn't seem to hear her, either. The retriever looked up at her, but didn't move.

Carlotta turned to her son. "Darren!" she ordered.

He stopped in the act of removing groceries from the bag and went to brush the dogs aside and lift Savannah onto his hip. Tippy, the terrier, took off around the table, with Spike in pursuit. Scarlett sat down beside Darren's feet, her tail still wagging.

"Hi, Savannah," he said, smiling into her suddenly uncertain expression. "I'm your uncle Darren. And this is Grandma Carlie."

Carlie put a hand up to the child's cheek and studied her.

Savannah returned her scrutiny, brown eyes wide. "Hi," she said.

"Guess what I brought you," Carlie challenged, holding up a shopping bag in her left hand.

Savannah leaned out of Darren's arms to peer into it. "What?"

Carlie reached into the bag and produced a soft stuffed rabbit in a flowered dress. The ears of three baby bunnies protruded from the pockets of an apron.

Savannah squealed with delight and hugged it to her. A friendship was made.

Libby smiled and felt the bite of emotion in her throat at their obvious pleasure in each other. Then it occurred to her that this charming little scene was completely counterproductive to the end result she was after.

And for the first time since she'd let Jared believe the nanny agency had sent her, she realized there were other feelings involved here besides her own. Jared's could be ignored because he was far less qualified than she was to be a parent.

But Carlie appeared to be great grandmother material. And Darren had taken the time to see that his brother's freezer contained food that would appeal to a child.

"Where *is* your daddy?" Carlie asked.

Savannah looked back at her with the fatalistic acceptance of a child powerless to change her fate. "In heaven," she said. "And Mommy, too."

Carlie closed her eyes for an instant, then brought the girl's little hand to her lips. "I know, sweetie. I'm sorry. But where's Jared?"

"Sleeping," Savannah replied.

Carlie cleared her throat. "Want to go get him and tell him Uncle Darren's going to make pancakes?"

Savannah looked pleased. "With blueberries?"

"With apples." Darren lowered her to her feet. "And whipped cream. Is that okay?"

She smiled widely. "Yeah. Be right back." She ran off toward the stairs.

Carlie put her coat and hat on the back of a chair and came to take Zachary from Libby.

Libby removed a tea towel from a decorative rack against the wall that held table linens and put it on Carlie's shoulder as they traded places. She was just about to explain that he'd just had a full meal, when Carlie placed him against her shoulder with obvious experience and began to burp him.

"Thank you, Libby," Carlie said. "Please don't think of me as endangering your job, I've just wanted grandchildren for so long. I'd love to hold him for a little while."

"Please do." Libby smiled down into sparkling hazel eyes. "I'll make some coffee. Are you comfortable?"

"Would you get one of the throw pillows on the sofa for my back?"

"You bet." Libby hurried off and returned with a red one sprigged with beige flowers and tucked it in the small of Carlie's back as she leaned forward.

"Old injury that's attracting arthritis in my old age." Carlie leaned back with a satisfied sigh. "Everyone else has to do my bending for me. Ah. Perfect."

Libby searched the cupboards for coffee.

Darren pointed a whisk toward the shelf just above the coffee maker. He'd removed his tuxedo jacket and worked with his sleeves rolled up, though the points of his collar curled over a black bow tie. He'd wrapped a white towel around his middle. "In there. Filters, too." He broke eggs with one hand, even managing to separate whites and yolks into different bowls. He whipped the whites with the skill of a master.

"May I ask you a question?" Libby fitted a filter in the coffee maker's basket and measured out coffee.

Darren glanced up from his task with a smile. "Of course."

"Have you been to a formal affair?" she inquired, indicating his attire, "or are you on your way?"

He laughed. "My staff's meeting at the photographer's at ten for pictures for my brochure. I always host in a tux."

That was a more logical explanation than she'd expected.

"One more question."

"Yes?"

"Why does only one dog have a leash attached?"

He turned to answer just as Tippy and Spike did one more lap around the table, barking in their excitement. As they passed Carlie's chair and ignored her order to stop, she slapped her black wedgie down on the end of the leash. The terrier was stopped in his tracks and flipped onto his back.

Libby gasped, but the dog, apparently accustomed to the maneuver, rolled onto his side and stood, wagging his tail at his mistress.

"Darren!" Carlie commanded.

Darren sighed with strained patience, then added quietly to Libby, "As Mom mentioned, she doesn't bend very well, and Tippy's completely out of control. That's the only way she has to catch him."

Darren took the end of the dog's leash and slipped it around the knob on the back door. He whipped up more eggs and milk, even added a dash of vanilla, then poured the mixture into three small bowls and set them against the back door.

Tippy dug in, and the other two dogs converged on the spot.

"Thank you, dear," Carlie said to Darren.

He grinned at Libby as he put a large frying pan on the stove and turned the heat on under it. "Sure, Mom."

JARED AWOKE to a slap in the face. Well, it wasn't a slap exactly, more like a sort of pounding applied to his right cheek, then, when he was too confused to respond, on his forehead.

Fortunately, he thought, as he struggled to surface from the remnants of a dream about fishing on the banks of Loch Broom, there wasn't much power behind whatever drove the weapon.

He opened his eyes just in time to stop a tiny hand from landing a blow on his nose. He blinked and discovered Savannah kneeling on his chest. She still wore her Pocahontas pajamas, but her eyes were large and bright and wide-awake.

"Come on!" she said excitedly. "There's a man making pancakes! And Grandma...Grandma Somebody gave me this!" She held up a stuffed rabbit wearing a dress. In the rabbit's apron pockets were three baby bunnies. "And there's puppies everywhere! Come on!" She scrambled off him and was gone.

He put a hand over his eyes and groaned, trying to brace himself for what lay ahead. His mother was here. Apparently she'd ignored his request for a few days to settle in. Or Darren hadn't passed it on. He could be cussed that way.

From beyond his open door, he heard the thump of dog feet on the carpeted stairs, then loud giggles when they intercepted Savannah on her way down.

He checked across the hall, found Zachary's crib empty, and concluded that Libby must already be up. He showered, shaved and dressed.

A cozy group was assembled in the kitchen when he got there. Libby stood at the stove with Zachary in her arms, laughing with his brother as he removed a golden, paper-thin crepe from a frying pan with a skilled flip.

His mother sat at the end of the table nearest them with Savannah in her lap. Each of them held one of the pocket bunnies and appeared to be manipulating them in conversation.

"The carrots are so poor this year," his mother said in an animated falsetto. "I just don't know what to have for breakfast."

Savannah wiggled her bunny from side to side and replied, "You can have one of my crops."

"Crepes," Darren corrected from the stove. "Like grapes, only cr-epes."

"You can have one of my crepes," Savannah amended.

"And some of your apple compote?"

Savannah shook her head. "I don't have apple compote."

"Sure you do." Darren served up a small bowlful from a pan on the stove, spooned up some and offered it to her.

She dutifully opened her mouth and took a taste. Her eyes gleamed. "Yummy." She held her little rabbit up to his mother's and said very seriously, "You can have a crepe, but the apple stuff is mine."

His mother laughed and hugged her.

"That smells wonderful," Libby said, inhaling the apple-and-spice aroma.

Jared watched Darren reach into the drawer behind him, extract a fork and spike up a slice of apple. He held it out to her and she took it off the fork with her teeth. Anger, ripe and completely unjustified, swelled inside him.

It was punctured an instant later when Savannah noticed him, squirmed off his mother's lap and came to him to take him by the hand and pull him into the room.

She pointed to his mother. "That's your mom!" she said, obviously pleased to know that. Then she pointed to Darren. "And he's your brother!"

"Very good," he said, lifting her onto his hip. "Good morning. Did you sleep well?"

"Uh-huh. We're gonna have pancakes with whipped cream!"

"That sounds...good." He added the last lamely, unable to think of anything that sounded worse at that hour. Savannah, however, seemed enthused.

Darren glanced at him over his shoulder. "Relax," he said. "I'm putting apple*jack* in yours and skipping the cream."

Jared felt relief. "Now you're talking."

His mother opened her arms for Savannah. He placed the child in her lap, then leaned down to kiss his mother's cheek.

"What a nice surprise, Mom," he said. He was sincerely glad to see her, but she openly admitted to a meddlesome nature, and he wasn't anxious to have her second-guessing his parenting skills at a time when he felt very much as though he didn't have any.

Then he remembered that she'd arrived at Darren's before he, Jared, had even gotten home from Scotland and decided to adopt the children. So, something else must have brought her here.

"What's taken you away from the shop?"

She heaved a deep sigh and shrugged a shoulder while hugging Savannah to her. "Maybe we can talk about it later?" she asked hopefully. "I have to leave this afternoon. Gertie sat in for me for a few days so I could come down, but she's expected in Bend for the weekend. I thought you were coming back last week. I didn't know about the..." Unwilling to upset Savannah, she didn't say the words. "You know."

He nodded.

"Darren was nice enough to put me up." She smiled at her younger son's back. "Did you know he has the Bad Boy Channel?"

Before he could reply, Darren turned away from the stove, a pancake turner waving accusingly in her direction. "How do *you* know I have it?" He forestalled her attempt to reply with a quick "Because you watched it your*self!*"

She tilted her chin indignantly. "I was trying to find CNN."

Darren snickered and turned back to his work.

"Did *you* sleep well?" Libby asked him as he took Zachary from her. She fixed him with an innocent stare, through which he could see a wealth of smugness. She added with all apparent concern, "Once you finally got to bed, I mean?"

His brother carried a platter to the table, which caused his mother to move Savannah to another chair while she hurried to help Darren with all the accompaniments.

Isolated at the end of the counter with Libby and the baby, Jared looked into her clear blue eyes and found that this morning, her impertinence intrigued him.

The night she'd hired on, and last night, her presumptions had annoyed him. But he'd thought about her in the wee hours of the morning while he'd slept fitfully, and decided that he found her reactions interesting.

She meant the children no harm; he was certain of that. That she cared for them was in her eyes, in the way she touched them, in the way she hovered, even when he was near.

So she must be governed by a need to discredit him, though he couldn't imagine why.

What did that all mean? Until he could figure it out, he didn't mind doing what he could to unsettle her self-satisfaction.

"Zack did keep me up quite a while," he admitted genially, dodging the baby's hand as Zachary slapped at his chin. He finally caught it and shook it playfully. "Why? Were you spying on me again?"

Her even look slipped just a little and for an instant he saw fear in her eyes. He knew she was recalling his threat about letting her go if he caught her watching him.

Curiously, the fear appeared very genuine. As though it involved more than her loss of a job. He wondered about that as she blinked and met his gaze again.

"No, I wasn't," she replied, her voice just a tad shaken. "My room is next to yours. I heard you."

"But I made a point of being quiet," he needled. "Were you listening for me?"

A little color crept into her cheeks. He found that curious, too.

"Of course not," she denied. "I was...I had a touch of insomnia."

"Guilty conscience for having spied on me the first time?"

Libby was beginning to get the feeling she was being toyed with. There was amusement in the dark depths of his eyes and a slightly arrogant indolence in the way he watched her.

"More likely, it was a reaction to intimidation by an unreasonable employer." She returned the half teasing, half serious accusation.

He tilted his head in a gently scolding manner. "You're trying to make me believe you're afraid of me?"

For an instant, before she could hide the truth in her eyes with another blink, they did betray fear of him. That so surprised him, particularly considering her rather forceful behavior on behalf of the children, that for a moment he was stunned.

Then Darren pulled a chair out and beckoned Libby to sit in it.

"Come on, come on," he ordered. "Both of you. I didn't get up at the crack of dawn to fix your breakfast just to have you let it get cold."

The crepes were delicious. Jared was happy to see that Savannah devoured them. Libby, on the other hand, ate one and toyed with the others, watching him surreptitiously when she thought he was distracted by his mother's conversation.

But he could *feel* her eyes on him. He thought he might even be haunted by that quick glimpse of fear he'd seen. He would certainly be plagued by the question of what the hell it meant.

Was her pugnacious attitude toward him an attempt to conceal some vulnerability his presence caused her?

That didn't make sense. She was the one who'd agreed to take the position. And who'd pleaded to maintain it twice.

Whatever her reservations toward him, she seemed delighted with his brother. That anger Jared had felt when he'd walked into the room tried to rise again, but he pounded it down with the clinical observation that if they found each other good company, it was not a problem for anyone. Particularly not for him.

It just felt as though it was.

"And so... I just don't know what to do about it. I mean, am I too old even to be thinking in those terms?" He came out of his thoughts, to find that his mother's earnest eyes were on him and that she was apparently coming to the end of a question he should have been paying closer attention to. "But then, the Chambers are very long-lived, you know. Your grandfather died at eighty-eight. I could have another twenty-five years. And if I can have them doing the tango—shouldn't I?''

The tango. He tried to clear his mind of all the personal complications of the past few days and concentrate on his mother. Though she sometimes exasperated him, she'd been a model mother, and still did her best to be understanding and supportive. There wasn't time enough to give back all she'd given him.

He placed his hand on the back of her chair and accorded her his full attention. "Clarify that for me," he said, trying to skirt the fact that he'd apparently missed a lot of what she'd told him.

She asked with a sigh, "You weren't listening, were you?"

"I was...distracted," he admitted, indicating the baby asleep in his carrier on the other side of him. "Tell me again. What was that about the tango?"

She opened her mouth to begin again, when the back door opened after a perfunctory knock.

"Hi!" Justine called, waving a white bag. "I stopped at the bakery on my way in. I thought Savannah—"

She proceeded two steps into the room, and fell over Tippy's leash as the dog strained across the opening to reach a small portion of milk and egg left in Spike's bowl. She almost caught her balance, but Spike shot past her out the open door and Tippy tried to follow, tripping her up again.

Libby and Carlie screamed as she landed with a crash, jarring the door and dislodging the loop of the terrier's leash, which was secured to the knob. He ran over her back and out the door in pursuit of his companion.

Libby, closer to the door, started toward her, but Darren reached her first. He lifted her to her feet, brushed down her short skirt and asked in concern, "Justy, are you all right?"

She stopped in the process of straightening her sweater and looked up into his eyes, her own going a little misty with recognition. "Darren," she said in soft surprise.

The next instant her gaze hardened and she shook off his supporting arm. "I'm quite all right, thank you. This must be what it's like being the rabbit at the dog races." She smiled wryly toward the table. "Hello, Carlie. Good morning, all."

Libby took Justine's arm and pulled her toward her chair. "Here, you sit down. I'll get you a cup of coffee."

Justine gave Darren a lethal look and hobbled along with her. "I can't stay. I just thought Savannah might like a doughnut for breakfast."

"That's a good way to instill the habit of having a nutritious breakfast," Darren grumbled, his manner changing from solicitousness to irritability. He pulled his jacket off the back of his chair.

Justine pointed to the whipped cream in the bottom of a bowl on the table. "I'm sure artery-clogging whipped cream sends a better message. Oh, do you have to go? Too bad." She added the last with grave insincerity.

He opened his mouth to reply, but Jared stood and walked him forcefully toward the door. "Thanks, Darren," he said, opening the door and pushing his brother through when he would have tried to turn back to have the last word. "I appreciate your fixing breakfast."

"Sure." Darren shrugged his tux jacket into place as they walked toward his gray Volvo station wagon. The good humor with which he'd made a second round of crepes had evaporated with the arrival of Justine. "I think you're nuts to take the kids, but they are beautiful, and being nuts doesn't seem to have stopped you from being successful with whatever you decide to do, so who am I to criticize?"

Jared jammed his hands in his pockets as Darren unlocked the tailgate. The day was crisp and clear, and the cold air from the ocean bit through his sweatshirt.

"You know, maybe you and Justy should try to settle this issue between you," he suggested.

"Why?" Darren asked coolly, lifting the door and revealing a pumpkin the size of a footstool. "That would be productive only if we wanted to salvage the relationship."

"Don't you?"

Darren reached into the back to drag the pumpkin forward. "Of course not. She's a shrew who has little interest in me except as a sperm bank."

Jared laughed. "Poor you."

Darren straightened and gave him a judicious look. "I appreciate a lusty woman as much as the next guy, but when it comes down to it, I'm not making babies I don't get to father."

"I understand that." Jared grew serious. "But what are you going to do about the fact that you still love her? And she loves you."

"If that were true," Darren said wearily, "wouldn't she *want* to marry me?"

"Her father was abusive. Deep down she probably thinks fathers—any fathers—are scary."

Darren put an emphatic hand to his own chest. "What in God's name is scary about me?"

Jared couldn't help another laugh. "You mean besides your preference for country-and-western music and your pre-Columbian mask collection?"

Darren closed his eyes and asked fervently, "Why do I even *try...?*"

"Because I saved you from Willy Goldbeck when you were eight. If I hadn't pulled you out of the trash compactor, you'd be part of some cardboard box made of recycled materials."

"Yeah, well, who let Mom believe that the cat and not her precious firstborn son broke that Zsolnay vase that was going to finance her trip to Europe?"

Jared nodded. "That was very heroic of you and I'll appreciate it till my dying day."

"Which could be looming on the horizon if you don't quit hassling me about Justy." Darren lifted the pumpkin with a groan and handed it to Jared.

"I'm not hassling you." Jared braced his feet to accept the weight. "I just think you'd both be better off if you fought it out, rather than sniping at each other every time you meet. What does this thing weigh?"

"Forty-two pounds. I thought Savannah might think it was fun. How's she doing?"

Jared inclined his head in a gesture of uncertainty. "I'm not sure. I don't know what she was like before. Sometimes she looks at me as though she's terrified of me, but last night she told me she liked me. So...we'll see what happens as time goes by."

Darren closed the tailgate and smiled suddenly. "The nanny was a good choice on your part."

"I didn't choose her," Jared denied. "I called the agency and they sent her over."

"Then you got really lucky."

"Maybe."

"What do you mean?"

Jared opened his mouth to explain, then decided he didn't know how. "Could we talk about this," he asked, "when I'm *not* holding a forty-two-pound pumpkin?"

Darren walked around to the driver's side door. "You need to build up those biceps. I'll be back for Mom after lunch. She left her car at my place."

"Thanks again for breakfast."

"Anytime."

LIBBY, HELPING CARLIE clear the table and load the dishwasher, glanced out the window at Jared and Darren standing near the Volvo. Jared was laughing and Darren looked disgusted with him—in a tolerant sort of way.

She envied them their relationship. She'd been raised without siblings and orphaned while still too young to feel truly secure within herself. She wondered what it was like to have someone you could call if you wanted to discuss a life-altering decision, or if you simply felt lonely or afraid.

She had Sara and Charlene, of course, but that wasn't like having someone who'd shared your life from infancy, and whose life was irrevocably tied to yours.

So, she usually made all her big decisions on her own. And if she felt lonely or afraid—she lived with it until she got over it.

"I wish Darren would sit Justine down and talk to her," Carlie said, "instead of engaging in this verbal barrage every time they see each other."

Savannah sat at the table with a coloring book and crayons Carlie had also brought.

Carlie settled herself at the other end of the table with the bag of apples and a peeler. "Would you fill that bowl with water and bring it to me, please?" She pointed to a yellow bowl on the top shelf. "And maybe the newspaper for the peelings." Her pointing finger moved to a folded paper near the phone. "How do you feel about Puerto Rico?"

Libby used a chair to climb onto the old counter and held on to a shelf with one hand to steady herself. "I've never been," she said, reaching overhead for the heavy bowl. "But I understand it's quite beautiful."

"I've never been, either." Carlie's voice went on behind her as Libby struggled to get a grip on the weighty bowl. It was very plain, but looked like something her grandmother might have used, and the last thing she wanted to do was drop it. "Julio wants to take me there."

"Julio?" Libby asked absently as she arched her back to lean the bowl against her chest so that she could wrap her arm around it. She was reluctant to let go of the shelf because the counter was narrow and her perch precarious.

"A customer who collects *azulejo*. But he's become more than that over the past few months." The sound of the peeler at work accompanied her story. "We go dancing all the time. We can't dip, of course, like that show-off Martha Gershoff and her husband, because of my back, but we have a wonderful time. We always close the place."

Libby turned in a small semicircle like a broken robot, the bowl in one arm, the shelf gripped in her other hand, when Spike raced through the kitchen with Tippy in pursuit. They ran under her chair, then around it as Scarlett, feeling rested and frisky, tried to head them off. They turned back and, with the leash wrapped around the legs of the chair, dragged it off.

"Ah..." Libby said, trying to get Carlie's attention.

But she was apparently lost in thoughts of Julio as she pared apples like a madwoman. "I told the boys I've been going dancing, but I didn't tell them that I was beginning to fall in love again. I mean, who thinks it'll happen again at sixty-nine? I was as surprised as anyone. But do I really want to turn my entire life around? And what would I do about the shop if I moved to Puerto Rico?"

"Move to Puerto Ri—!" Jared sounded shocked, then he cut off as he closed the kitchen door behind him and saw Libby standing on the counter, clinging to the shelf. He came to stand under her, hands on his hips. "What are you doing?"

"I'm practicing to tackle Everest," she said, annoyed that he seemed annoyed. "I intend to leave a bowl for offerings at the summit."

He shifted his weight, his eyes berating her smart reply.

"I asked her to get me a bowl," Carlie said. "No need to be testy with her."

"Really? You want to explain on the insurance claim how she fractured three limbs and her head?" He reached up for the bowl and placed it on the table. "When you asked her to get the bowl, you might have told her there was a step stool in the mudroom." Then he reached up for Libby. "Come on. Get off there. How did you get up there, anyway?"

She wanted more than anything at that moment to have the ability to flutter down to the floor on her own. She didn't want to have to touch him. She didn't want to have to let him touch her.

"I used a kitchen chair," she replied coolly, pointing with the hand now blessedly free of the bowl to the spot across the room where the dogs played. Tippy was still wrapped around the chair. "They dragged it away."

He closed his eyes for a moment, then beckoned her with his fingertips. "Come on. Put your hands on my shoulders."

She did it, her teeth gritted against the contact. He was everything that stood in her way. He was smug and judgmental, and sometimes, when she turned and found him watching her, she wondered if he wasn't onto her— or at least wondering what she was up to.

She expected everything she so disliked about him to transfer itself to her when she touched him.

What she experienced was entirely different. The instant she braced her hands on his shoulders and his hands gripped her waist, she felt warmth, muscle, competence and a paradoxical sense of safety. How that could be when he presented a threat to everything she wanted, she didn't know; but she felt it all the same.

He swung her off the counter and that sharp, startling realization made the small move feel as though it took an eternity. She looked into his eyes and saw reflected there the same strange timelessness she felt.

She'd been held by men before, but the contact had had the feel of a very contemporary communication. She'd always appreciated being on an equal footing with a man, but she didn't quite have that here. His hands were in charge. His muscle was supporting her. But she was being held protectively, her needs of the moment superseding his, so that for an instant she felt as though she'd gone one hundred years back in time rather than ten. And she had the feeling of not being equal at all, but very special.

When he finally put her down she fought an alarming need to hold on.

Jared couldn't seem to take his hands off her. He could feel the fragility of her rib cage under his fingers, the swell of the underside of a breast under his thumb.

His nostrils were filled with her heady floral fragrance and did not seem to be taking in air. He looked into her eyes and experienced a disorienting weightlessness usually associated with asphyxiation or drowning. He could feel her heart thudding against his thumb.

Then her feet touched the floor and he felt suddenly as though he, too, had landed.

She dropped her hands from his shoulders and said a polite thank-you.

He tried to stabilize his heartbeat as she went to the telephone table and returned with a paper she handed his mother. She sat opposite her, picked up a small paring knife and began to peel apples.

He had no idea what that had been all about. Enforced celibacy, he guessed, during four weeks abroad. Like Darren, he enjoyed a lusty woman as much as the next guy, but he'd never been ruled by desire.

He rationalized it as a result of the pressures of the past few days, then dismissed it.

He went to sit beside his mother and take the peeler from her.

"Puerto Rico?" he demanded, trying to pretend that that unsettling little interlude hadn't happened. "What do you mean? Why? With whom?"

"I mean San Juan," she replied quietly. She always did that when she'd driven him to the point of apoplexy. "Because I've been invited to go. By Julio Ruiz, my dear friend. Not that I have to explain myself to you."

He was beginning to see the light. "So, that's why you came."

"I came," she said, glancing up at him over her glasses as she polished an apple with the sleeve of an elegant black blouse, "because I wanted to see my new grandchildren. You and your brother do seem to be cases of arrested development in the area of forming the permanent attachments required to make families."

"You came to Darren's," he stated, "*before* you heard about your grandchildren."

She cast him another look that scolded without actually denying the truth of what he said. "It isn't nice to correct your mother," she said.

"So, maybe you *should* explain yourself to me." He took the apple from her and put it aside. "Preferably *before* you end up on a tropical island sporting ruffles and a bare midriff."

She laughed at the notion, then sobered again and admitted with a deep sigh, "I'm in love, Jared. And I think I'm going to be married."

He did his best to take the news with equanimity, then tried to imagine how his father would have handled the situation. The man had always seemed able to deal with her. "No, you're not," he said with the quiet voice his father had always used that suggested death would result if his wishes were thwarted.

She met his eyes, her own sparking. "Don't forget who was in labor with whom for thirty-one hours."

He heard Libby draw a breath to offer an opinion, but he fixed her with a look intended to freeze the words on her lips.

She arched an eyebrow at him, obviously not intimidated. "Shouldn't you know a little about him before *you* determine your mother's future?"

His father, he decided, must have dealt with a different breed of woman.

"You're not marrying anyone," he said firmly to his mother, "before Darren and I have met him. What does he do? What are his . . . his . . . ?"

"Prospects?" Carlie asked with a wry smile. "Retirement benefits, I believe. He's with the Puerto Rico Bureau of Tourism. He used to be an entertainer and now he's a sort of goodwill ambassador. He has a tidy savings account."

"An entertainer," Jared repeated flatly. "Mom, what's happened to the levelheaded woman who won't even buy an iffy stock? Is this . . ." He waggled a hand, unable to find a word he was willing to say to his mother.

She and Libby exchanged a look that made him feel completely alien.

"Sexual?" his mother inquired. "You bet. He's gorgeous. And every time he kisses me, I feel like a bride again."

He was horrified. "What? Don't you listen to the warnings? Haven't you heard about . . . ?"

"My *interest,*" she interrupted a little loudly, "is sexual as well as intellectual and spiritual and emotional. But both of us grew up in a time when we respected those things and held them only for each other. And we've done that. What am I, sixteen?"

"I don't know," he replied a little hotly, "you sound a little hormonal to me."

She laughed. "Darling, my estrogen comes out of a bottle these days. I *love* this man, but I came to you because I am afraid of changing everything, of moving farther away from you and Darren, and I wanted you to reassure me that no matter what, you'll always love me and support what I choose to do.''

Her little speech made him feel like a heel. Libby's glance from across the table rubbed it in. He decided to hold firm.

"I will always love you, no matter what," he said earnestly, "but I can't support something that could ultimately hurt you—unless you can convince me it won't. So bring Julio down to meet us."

"He wants to go home the first of December," she said, her gaze sliding away from his.

"So, you'd be gone for Christmas?" he asked defensively. He couldn't imagine Christmas without her. Since his father's death, he and Darren had always made it to her home for Christmas, no matter how far away they'd been. "Now that you have grandchildren?"

"She could bring him down for Thanksgiving," Libby suggested.

Carlie looked at him hopefully.

He couldn't think of one reason that wouldn't work out—though he intended to have a word with the intrusive Miss Madison. Julio. An entertainer, no less. He imagined ruffled sleeves and maracas.

"Sure. Let's do that," he said, hiding the reluctance with which he agreed. "Thanksgiving here."

Carlie smiled and pulled him toward her over the edge of the table to kiss his cheek. "Thank you. I knew you could be reasonable. If you let me have the peeler back, I can have apple pies in the freezer before Darren comes back for me."

CARLIE ROCKED Zachary while her pies baked, then she colored with Savannah and left on schedule after hugging everyone.

"See you at Thanksgiving," she promised as Darren closed her into the car.

"Am I gonna paint now?" Savannah asked as the car turned out of the driveway and onto the road. She looked up at Jared, an expectant smile in place. "You said I could paint today."

He turned to Libby, the baby in his left arm. "Do you have all the paints you'll need?"

She knew she was on thin ice with him for taking his mother's side, so she tried to smile pleasantly. "Yes, I do. I made a few sketches last night before I went to bed. Would you like to approve them before we start?"

His dark eyes widened dramatically as he held the door open for them to go back into the house. "You'd like my opinion? How novel."

She shooed Savannah toward the stairs. "Go change into the jeans with the torn knee, okay? And that old Mickey Mouse sweatshirt."

Savannah raced upstairs to comply.

Libby turned to her employer, thinking that she really had to assume a more subservient role if she was going to get anywhere with this man, but she kept finding herself in situations that made it difficult. She tried to recall if she'd been less impulsive ten years into the future, but couldn't remember.

It was a strange concept, she thought absently, trying to remember the future.

"I know your mother's affairs are none of my business," she said frankly but reasonably, "but I related to her instantly. She looked so alone and afraid when you came on so disapproving. I thought she could use someone on her side.''

''Maybe you related to her,'' he said, moving Zachary into his other arm. He turned her toward the stairs and held her elbow as they climbed, the chivalrous gesture at odds with the chewing out. ''But you've known her all of six or seven hours. I've known her all my life.''

''Yes, but in all that time, you've never been able to think likc a woman to understand what she's feeling.''

He couldn't deny that, so he looked for another point to dissect. ''She's lived most of her life in Seattle! Now she wants to go to Puerto Rico? With an entertainer?''

''You mean it's all right for you to go to Scotland and wherever else you've been in the interest of your work, but she has to stay in one place?''

''I didn't go to Scotland to get married.''

''No, but you came home and made an instant decision to take in two little children, and I didn't hear *her* climb all over *you* for making a drastic change in your life.''

He expelled an exasperated sigh as they topped the stairs. Zachary frowned at him, his little bow mouth moving as though he had an opinion he'd like to share if only he could.

Jared patted the baby's back, thinking how good it would be when he was old enough to offer a second male point of view.

''Mom has her shop,'' he said, ''her friends, Darren and me. She's been happy. Why take a chance like that?''

''Why do you think she travels everywhere with three dogs?'' she asked gravely. ''I think she needs someone. If she loved your father, she's probably more lonely without him than she'd ever admit to you. And people who had a good first marriage are more likely to find a second permanent partner. Don't you get lonely?"

He followed her down the hallway, which was lit by a leaded glass window at the far end. She turned at the door to her room to await his answer. He didn't have one. Not one he'd admit to, in any case. He hadn't been lonely a day in his life until he'd met Mandy. And he hadn't felt whole since the day she'd told him she loved Frank.

"I'm never lonely," he lied.

She smiled thinly, a vulnerability in the gesture that was sharply at odds with her buttinsky disposition. "Good for you," she said, turning away from him to push the door open into her room. "I'm lonely all the time. The sketch is over here on the drafting table."

He followed her into the tidy room and looked over her shoulder as she pointed to the paper pinned to the board. "This is Rosie..." She indicated a young, winged female figure in what was probably a night-gown, floating over the rooftops and spires of a city— Paris, he guessed, judging by a stylized version of the Eiffel Tower. Flying behind her, also winged, was a black-and-white cat. The whole of her design was trapped in a border about four inches deep. She pointed to the cat. "And this is Tux."

He nodded. "They have *croissants* at the *boulangerie* and visit the Louvre, as I recall. And go home on the Concorde. You've been to Paris?"

"Only in my dreams." She pointed to rooftops and enumerated the places they represented. "I'll do different cities on different walls. London, Rome, New York. And except for a bottom drawer that Savannah can work on, I'll just do a border so that..." She stopped herself from saying aloud, *So that when you can't deal*

*with the children after all and agree to let me take them,
all you'll have to do is repaint the upper five inches of
wall and pretend you never made the mistake of thinking you could parent.*

"So that..." she said aloud, "if you don't like it, it'll
be easy to repaint. And it won't intrude on whatever
you had planned for decor."

"I hadn't planned anything, really," he said. "Her
toys are coming along with a shipment of architectural
details I sent from Scotland. So I thought we'd just wait
until those arrive and do what she wants."

"All right. Then we'll get busy." She pointed to a
deep bottom drawer across the room. "I'll sketch that
for Savannah to paint while I work along the top."

"Can you manage that and Zachary, too?"

"Sure. I'll be working in fits and starts anyway. I'll
bring the carrier up to make him comfortable. I think
he'll be fine as long as he can see us."

"Okay." He studied her an extra moment. "I'm going to spend the rest of the afternoon in the workshop.
If you need anything, there's an intercom down the hall
in my room, and one downstairs in the kitchen near the
phone. Press the button to signal me, press the bar to
talk, then let it go to hear my answer."

"Right."

Savannah ran into the room, dressed just as Libby
had suggested, except that the shirt was on backward
and the tag stuck out of the neck under her delicate
chin.

"I'm ready!" she said excitedly, jumping in place.

Jared handed Libby the baby, dropped laughingly to
one knee and pulled Savannah in front of him. "Well,
how's Mickey supposed to see what you're doing when
he's behind you," he teased, raising her arms so that he

could pull the shirt off her. He held up the tag. "See this? It goes in the back."

He pulled it over her head again and tugged it back down. Then, in an artlessly tender gesture, he brushed the baby-fine dark hair out of her face with the tips of his fingers.

She giggled.

Libby felt a stab of barbed guilt.

He kissed Savannah's cheek, stood and chucked Zachary under the chin, then turned to the door. "I'll bring the carrier up before I go."

"Am I sappose to call him 'Daddy' now?" Savannah asked as his footsteps sounded on the stairs.

Libby felt the answer catch in her throat. But the little girl needed a sense of security, of a situation that wouldn't change. She felt at a loss.

"Do you want to call him 'Daddy'?" was a convenient evasion.

Savannah shrugged. "He doesn't look like my other one."

That was the point, Libby thought righteously. She would want to call him "Daddy" if he *felt* like a daddy. Of course she knew that kind of bond couldn't be forged over a matter of days, but it helped fortify her own position.

"Well, you only have to call him 'Daddy' if you want to."

"Are you 'Mommy'?"

She wanted nothing more in the world than to reply with a hearty yes. But instead she had to say, at least for now, "I'm just Libby, the nanny."

"What *is* a nanny?"

"A lady who takes care of children."

"But that's what mommies do."

"Nannies," Libby explained patiently as she lay Zachary on her bed so that she could quickly change her shirt, "take care of children when there isn't a mommy around."

"Like 'cause she died," Savannah said rather matter-of-factly.

"Yes," Libby said, trying to sound calm, when in truth the child's acceptance broke her heart. "But sometimes mommies who are really busy hire nannies to take care of the children when they're at work." She yanked an old blue sweater out of a dresser drawer, willing to sacrifice it to the cause of Savannah's border. "Remember Dr. Brown who fixed the cut on your arm when you were in the hospital?"

"Yeah."

"She has a nanny."

"Oh." Apparently bored with the subject, Savannah wandered across the room to the built-in closet and drawers. "What am I gonna paint?"

"That drawer on the bottom. The big one."

Savannah knelt in front of it, pulled it open and peered inside.

Libby took advantage of the moment of quiet to pull off her good sweater. Then she turned to the foot of her bed for the old blue one, and stopped stock-still at the sight of Jared in the doorway, the baby's carrier hanging by its handle in his hand.

She held the sweater up to her chest, but not before she spent a full five seconds simply staring at him in stunned surprise.

His dark eyes swept over her blush lace bra and lingered for a moment.

Her heart thudded. His eyes lifted to hers and held. She couldn't speak or even breathe. That timeless quality was in control again.

He finally moved to place the carrier on the foot of the bed. Then he reached toward Libby. She leaped nimbly aside, only to redden in embarrassment when she saw that he was reaching for Zachary and not for her.

She yanked the sweater on as he placed the baby in the carrier.

"I did tell you I was coming back," he said, rattling Zachary's key toy. The baby extended a hand toward it and he let him take the toy, then straightened. His expression was indeterminate.

She folded her arms over her chest, as though that would somehow erase the image he'd seen. "I know. That was my fault. I'm sorry I embarrassed you."

"Embarrassed." He repeated the word consideringly, then growled a laugh. "That doesn't describe what I felt at all." He crossed the room to Savannah, who now sat in the deep drawer, her bony knees folded up as she looked about herself in anticipation.

He rubbed the top of her head. "Be good for Libby. I'll see you at dinner."

He disappeared into the hall and Libby felt air rush into her body, as if she'd been holding her breath all that time.

Her cheeks were hot; her heart thumped erratically; and she would have been perfectly happy to have a drawer *she* herself could climb into and pull closed behind her.

Chapter Five

The weekend. Jared faced it with trepidation. He didn't fear being unable to deal with the children. He knew their learning to coexist would be a gradual thing, and that his role as father was simply to behave as though he had the answer to everything, even if he didn't.

He'd been sixteen before he'd understood that that was how his father operated. His mother had had emergency gall-bladder surgery, and Jared had been completely shocked to find his father distraught in the face of her pain, and lost without her presence in the house.

Darren had cooked, and Jared had run errands and taken care of other details until Carlie came home two weeks later.

He remembered the impact on his own self-confidence of learning that his father was human. The man had always seemed just short of divine. For the young man who wanted to emulate him, it had come as such a relief to know that he had vulnerabilities.

What Jared did fear that weekend was that Libby would see him being less than perfect. He had a feeling she'd be less forgiving of his vulnerabilities than he'd been of his father's.

He didn't even care at that point in time what motivated her. He just wanted to get through the weekend without having to ask her for help.

He took off in the car with the children Saturday morning, thinking a new perspective would be good for all of them. It was another crisp, cold day, and he had Savannah and Zachary bundled up accordingly and safely strapped into their car seats.

It occurred to him when they were halfway to town that he'd forgotten Zachary's pacifier, but the baby seemed cheerful and happy, and Jared decided to take the chance that he'd be all right without it.

He let Savannah push Zachary's stroller down the street as they walked the length of Cranberry Harbor's three-block-long main street, then up the other side, stopping to admire the wares in the window.

They checked in at ARCHI-JUNK, but Justy was helping an older gentleman who seemed to be considering the purchase of several chinoiserie panels he'd rescued from a brothel in San Francisco, so they moved on.

They had doughnuts at the bakery, and Savannah insisted that they sit outside at a small, round table on the sidewalk.

"Won't you be cold?" Jared asked.

"No." She walked on importantly, carrying her sugar doughnut and cup of juice. "Come on!" And led the way outside.

He sat opposite her and tucked Zachary's blanket in a little tighter.

Savannah's nose and her cheeks were bright pink, and her dark bangs fluttered under the red woolen hat tied under her chin. She looked around her with interest, her little legs swinging back and forth, hitting his knee with every pass.

She smiled happily at Jared. "We're just like Rosie and Tux," she said, pointing to herself and her baby brother.

Jared wondered what Zachary would think of being considered a counterpart to a cat.

"'Cept Rosie doesn't got a daddy."

Did that mean Savannah considered that she had? He was surprised at the degree to which that thrilled him.

"Libby says I don't got to call you 'Daddy.'"

He felt instant annoyance replace the thrill.

"Only if I want," she added.

Annoyance faltered in the face of fairness. It was certainly true that she didn't have to say or feel anything that wasn't genuine. And Libby had done nothing wrong in telling her so. Except that he was sure she'd enjoyed doing it.

"That's right," he said.

"But I forgot your name again," she admitted.

"Jared," he supplied.

"Where's Libby?" she asked suddenly.

Annoyance rose again. Not at the child, but at the woman the child was so fond of. The woman who seemed to make his brain stall when she got too close. The woman whose lace-covered breasts he'd dreamed about like some obsessed adolescent.

The woman whose presence in his home he didn't entirely trust for reasons he couldn't quite define.

"Today is her day off," he answered. "*She* gets to play today."

Savannah looked stricken. "Did she go away?"

"No," he reassured her quickly. "She just gets to relax today. She probably went shopping or something."

"Will she be home when we get home?"

"I don't know. Maybe."

"When will she play with me again?"

"On Monday."

"When's Monday?"

"Day after tomorrow."

She sighed, apparently willing to accept that if not entirely pleased with it.

During the next few hours, Jared discovered the difficulty of having one child who could not be put down and another who could not be let out of his sight.

In a shop filled with shiny bric-a-brac Savannah insisted on exploring, he carried Zachary in one arm and tried hard to control Savannah with the other. But the aisles were narrow and her fingers so quick that the experience was a nightmare.

He owned a hundred-dollar clock with a broken hand before he knew what happened.

Savannah stood glued to his side as the woman behind the counter wrapped the clock. It was made of wood in a whimsical, primitive style and shaped like a birdhouse. On top of it was a black-and-white cat reaching for a bird peering into the house. The bird had also broken off when the clock had fallen to the floor.

"Children should be taught to keep their hands in their pockets," the clerk said when she accepted his check.

He resented the affront to Savannah's innocent curiosity and his own meager but budding parenting skills. He wanted to tell her that shopkeepers who made it impossible for an adult to move through a shop had their brains in their pockets, but he resisted.

Outside, he put Zachary back in the stroller and stuffed the clock into the carry bag behind it. Savannah looked guilty and uncertain.

Zachary screamed at having been put down, and Jared had no pacifier with which to quiet him. So he lifted Savannah into one arm and pushed the stroller toward the car. "Next time," he said gently, "if you want to look at something, I'll get it down for you, okay? That way we won't break anything. If we break it, then the lady who owns the shop can't sell it."

Her expression turned from penitence to puzzlement. "She selled it to *us.*"

"I know, but we didn't really want it. We just bought it because we broke it."

Her puzzlement increased. "I want it."

Of course she did. That was why she'd wanted to look at it.

"But we already have a clock in your room. And we wouldn't have bought this one if we hadn't broken it."

Her eyes brimmed with tears. "Do you still like me?"

He kissed her cheek. "Of course I do." But he didn't like the clock.

She wrapped an arm around his neck and leaned into him.

Suddenly the clock didn't matter.

Zachary screamed all the way home, and Savannah talked nonstop over him. It was all a learning experience, Jared told himself philosophically. He'd never forget Zachary's pacifier again.

He opened the kitchen cupboard where he'd seen Libby find one more than once, but couldn't spot it.

Savannah pointed to a small plastic container on the bottom shelf. "Binkies are in that little cup thing," she said.

She was right.

"She puts hot water on it first."

He did that, then put it in Zachary's mouth. The baby spit it out angrily and continued to scream.

Jared half expected to hear Libby come running down the stairs with that superior expression on her face. In fact, he hoped she would. But she didn't. The house was quiet—except for Zachary.

He hooked the pacifier on his finger and went into the living room. He would have liked to build a fire, but that would have involved putting Zachary down, and he was afraid that if the baby screamed any louder he'd choke.

So he settled for turning up the thermostat for the oil furnace, and heard the comforting swell of sound as it kicked on.

Savannah dropped her coat and hat in the middle of the floor. "Can we have cocoa?"

"Sure," he said. "As soon as Zachary quiets down. Pick up your stuff and take it upstairs, please."

"Okay." She complied amenably.

Now, if he could just quiet Zachary, he'd feel as though it had been a fairly productive morning. The clock thing had been relatively minor, and Savannah had seemed to have a good time at the bakery. All in all, his first morning as a solo father hadn't gone badly.

He sat in the rocker with the baby, who now seemed inconsolable. His mouth was wide open in acute distress. Jared tried once more to insert the pacifier, but Zachary refused to close his mouth over it.

"I'm not giving up on you," he told the baby, smoothing his bald head with the tips of his fingers. It was warm and downy. "We've got to build a relationship here, buddy, because Savannah's pretty pushy and the nanny's definitely got a mind of her own. I need another male vote.''

Jared rubbed a fist across his eyes. The tone of his screeches lowered subtly.

Jared tried anew with the pacifier. This time Zachary took it and held it. The noise stopped as though a switch had been flipped. Quiet enveloped the room. Jared closed his eyes and wondered why he'd never appreciated before how blissful stillness was.

He opened his eyes again to see Zachary's drift closed. He continued to rock as the baby finally fell into a deep sleep.

He studied the little face feature by feature and thought he looked angelic, like the cherubs he'd once seen in a high-relief French mantelpiece.

So. He hadn't been able to have Mandy, but he had her children. There was some kind of poetic justice in that. He felt as if a rent in his life had been closed, a hollow had begun to fill.

He listened to the quiet sounds of the furnace, the clock, cars passing on the road—then he sat up with a start. Savannah. He couldn't hear her.

He put the baby back in the carrier, breathed a prayer of gratitude when he remained asleep and ran lightly up the stairs, trying not to jostle him.

"Savannah?" he called quietly from halfway up the stairs.

She didn't answer. He topped the stairs and turned down the hall, thinking in a panic that she could have climbed out a window, swallowed aspirin, stuck her finger in a socket!

He found her door partially open and pushed his way in, calling her name urgently. "Savannah!"

"Yeah?" she replied.

He stopped in relief in the middle of her room. She sat cross-legged in the window seat, above which Libby worked at the top of a ladder.

Libby turned at the sight of him, her brush poised in midair, her forearm braced against the wall to steady herself.

His eyes went instantly to the seat of a pair of old sweats she wore that bagged around her taut, round buttocks, failing to diminish their curving appeal. The snug sweater he remembered from the afternoon he'd walked in on her changing into it.

Her hair was caught back in a high, saucy ponytail, and there was a smudge of blue down the left side of her jaw.

"Hi," she said. "I'm sorry if we alarmed you. Savannah said you knew she was up here."

"It's all right." He placed the carrier on Savannah's bed and moved closer to admire Libby's work. Over the past few days she'd completed the border on two walls and was halfway along the window-seat wall with the Rosie and Tux figures. "I didn't know you were up here. I thought you might have gone somewhere for the day."

"You said I didn't *have* to leave."

"You don't." He walked along under the border she now worked on, and identified the Empire State Building, the Triborough Bridge and Times Square. A background of darkness and starlight alternated with rays of sunlight and little bluebirds in flight. He pointed to a large storefront he didn't recognize that had what appeared to be animals in the windows. "What's that?" he asked.

"F. A. O. Shorts," Savannah replied importantly.

"Schwartz," Libby corrected, enunciating. "The toy store."

He smiled. He couldn't help it. Libby's images were warm and whimsical, and though they occupied only the four or five top inches of the room, they lent it a charming fantasy that intrigued him. He could imagine what they did for Savannah.

He suddenly saw the troublesome nanny from a new perspective. She had undeniable talent, and he wouldn't be surprised at all if the publisher to whom she'd sent her manuscript and illustrations snapped her up and signed her to a multiple-book contract.

Which brought him back to what she was doing in his home in the first place.

She needed a job to keep her going while she waited to hear from the publisher. That made sense. But it was a little curious that she'd known the children before. Her explanation of having met them at the hospital where she volunteered for story hour was reasonable, yet the whole situation somehow refused to fit together comfortably for him.

He guessed it was her possessiveness with the children. Shouldn't nannies who moved around and eventually moved on be trained to guard against that?

But would a family want a nanny who didn't care deeply about the children in her charge?

He decided he was going in circles and dismissed the issue from his thoughts. Sunlight poured through the drapeless windows, Zachary was sound asleep and Savannah was smiling. All was well with his world for the moment.

"You're doing a beautiful job," he praised. "I'll have to compensate you for this."

"No, you don't." She turned back to her work. "This relaxes me. It's how I choose to spend my free time." While she talked, the brush in her hand executed a perfect little star.

"We gots a clock!" Savannah said excitedly, standing up on the window seat and peering up, leaning on the bucket shelf on Libby's ladder to brace herself.

Libby's tray of paints on the shelf tottered dangerously.

Jared moved quickly to steady child and paints. He lifted Savannah off the seat and onto the floor.

"No standing on the window seat," he said. "I don't want you to fall through the window. And if you lean on Libby's ladder, you'll tip her over. Come on and help me with the cocoa. You can show Libby the clock downstairs."

"Can she have cocoa, too?"

"Of course." He noticed that Libby looked uncertain. "Do you like cocoa?"

"Well, yes. But . . . you know . . . I don't want to intrude."

He studied her expression for signs of meddling or insincerity, but could find none. Perhaps she was truly concerned about not being in the way on a Saturday.

"With or without marshmallows?" he asked.

She smiled. That, he was sure, was genuine. It had to be. It was making his pulse thump.

"With."

"All right. Ten minutes." He picked up the carrier, caught Savannah's hand and headed downstairs.

LIBBY LOOKED OVER the clock as Savannah excitedly told the story of her morning in Cranberry Harbor.

"We had sugar doughnuts just like Rosie!"

"At a Scandinavian bakery rather than a *boulangerie,*" Jared translated.

"And there was this biiiiig—" her little hands stretched way out to each side "—street with stores on it."

"Not the Champs-Élysées. Front Street."

"That's where the clock was."

"I don't know what the name of it is, but it wasn't F. A. O. Schwartz."

"I dropped it and we had to pay for it." Savannah added that with a note of chagrin. Then she smiled across the table at Jared. "But he didn't yell at me, and he still likes me."

Libby saw in the child's manner how much more comfortable she'd grown with Jared over the past few days. She also saw how gentle and sincere he was with her, how patient with the baby, how willing he was to extend himself to see that they were comfortable and secure. She'd heard Zachary squalling, and Jared's quiet voice, talking to him.

She didn't like the way it was complicating her position, but as someone who loved the children, she couldn't ignore the benefits to them.

So she tried not to think about the ultimate results of those developing relationships and tried to concentrate on the moment.

"This should be easy to repair," she said. "And I can match the paint on the bird to fix that nick."

He sat back in his chair, one ankle resting on the other knee. He looked relaxed and somehow satisfied as he nodded. "I know it can be fixed," he said with a disparaging grimace. "I just thought it was kind of cutesy."

"Well, we like cutesy, don't we, Savannah? We'll put it in your room and move that plain round one."

Savannah applauded the idea. Her cocoa finished, she came around the table to climb into Jared's lap. Libby saw the indulgent smile in his eyes as he settled her comfortably in the crook of his arm.

"What are we gonna do now?" Savannah asked. She yawned hugely.

"What do you want to do?"

"Can we go swimming?"

"Too cold."

"Do you have a merry-go-round?"

"No. Sorry."

She sighed and leaned sideways to rest her head against his chest.

"Do you have movies?"

"You want to see *East of Eden* with James Dean?"

She sat up, puzzled. "What's that?"

He laughed, pulled her head back to his chest and kissed the top of her head. "I was teasing you. I don't have any kids' movies, but we'll have to get some. Want to see if you can find cartoons on television?"

"Okay. Can I do the clicker?"

"Sure. The Disney Channel is on twenty-six."

She slid off his lap and frowned. "I don't know two-number numbers. Can you find it?"

"Sure." He followed her into the living room and Libby eavesdropped on their conversation as she finished her last sip of hot chocolate.

"Two-number numbers," he told her, "are just two one-number numbers. Like this one is made up of two and six."

Libby had to think about that a minute, but Savannah seemed to grasp it immediately.

"Oh, yeah. That one and that one."

"Right. So you press two, and then you press six, and you get channel twenty-six."

There was a moment's silence, then a happy squeal as the sounds of a cheerful ditty came from the television.

Libby found herself smiling at Savannah's success. Then she groaned and dropped her head onto her folded arms as she realized Jared's progress with the children was a cause for anguish and not joy.

If he won them over, she lost. She couldn't take *happy* children away from their environment.

"What's the matter?"

Jared's concerned voice just above her made her raise her head in alarm. She had to remember her place, the scam, her pose.

But that was hard to do when he was bent over her so solicitously, his large, warm hand on her back, his eyes dark and kind.

"Ah...nothing," she said. "Just...stiff. My arms are stiff from raising them over my head." She rotated her shoulders to add credibility to her story. "I'm fine really."

He sat at a right angle to her and studied her face, as though trying to read the truth there. She couldn't seem to let her eyes settle on his. They were nice. She didn't want to know that.

"Want a couple of Ibuprofen?" he asked.

"No, thanks." She smiled and knew she looked nervous. "I've got to get back to work."

"It's your day off."

"I know. But I'd like to get that done."

"There's no hurry, is there?"

It was weird that she felt as though there was. The pressure of time had been building over the past few days, though she didn't understand why. She began to wonder if everyone who lied felt that way. Maybe it was the feeling that one could be exposed at any moment that created a sense of urgency.

"No. But when the light changes..." She shrugged. "It's harder to work." She stood, thinking she had to get away from him. Those eyes were reading her thoughts; she knew it.

He drew back. "Then go ahead," he said. "It's your day."

Late in the afternoon, Libby went downstairs to make a sandwich and brought it back upstairs with her so that she wouldn't have to have dinner with Jared and the children.

It would be good for him, she thought, to see what it was it like to try to eat while feeding a baby and a four-year-old. After a whole day of dealing with the children on his own, this could very well put him over the edge. She hoped so. Or so she told herself.

The real truth was, she was beginning to feel serious pangs of conscience. When she wasn't harassing him, he was very kind to her. And he was doing well with the children. She was beginning to feel a certain empathy with him that was sharply at odds with what she'd come here to do.

But there was no way she was relinquishing her claim to them. She had to have them. That had to be the point! Otherwise, why would she have been brought back in time to the day she'd been supposed to claim them?

So what did she do now? She had no idea. And she didn't want to have to sit across the table from him while she struggled with her options.

She turned the light on in the room at four and kept painting. Through the window, she saw swiftly moving clouds darken the sky and threaten a change of weather overnight.

Savannah did not reappear, and Libby guessed Jared was protecting her day off by keeping the child downstairs.

She cleaned up about eight, knowing Jared would be bringing Savannah up soon for a bath before bed. She carried the ladder and her paints into her own room and closed the door.

The room's proportions seemed small suddenly. Even confining. She went to her drafting table for something to do to while away the rest of the evening, then decided that her creative self needed a rest after the long day she'd put in.

She turned on the small television tucked into a shelf in the corner of her room, pulled off her paint-spattered clothes and dropped them into the bottom of her closet. She wrapped herself in a pink velour robe and lay on the bed to stretch her cramped muscles. It took her a circuit of the channels to find something she wanted to watch, then her eyes drifted closed. The last thing she remembered was Cindy Crawford advertising kissable lipstick.

"SHE WON'T talk to me," Savannah complained to Jared with a pout as he tossed her blankets back. She'd run across the hall to say good-night to Libby and appeared crestfallen.

"Maybe she fell asleep," Jared said, putting a finger to his lips to remind her to keep her voice down. Zachary was asleep in the crib.

Savannah looked at him impatiently as she climbed into bed. "She's bigger than me. She can stay up late!"

"I see." He fluffed her pillows and tucked her in. "But you know, sometimes adults like to go to bed early. Especially when they've worked really hard. And she did a lot of painting in here today."

Savannah smiled. "Yeah." She pointed to the Rosie character on the wall opposite her. "That's Rosie." Her finger moved to the cat. "And Tux. And that's the . . . the tower thing."

"The Eiffel Tower," Jared said.

"Yeah. I always forget that." Then she smiled into his eyes. "But I know your name now."

"Oh, yeah?" he challenged gently, kneeling beside her bed. "What is it?"

"It's Jared."

"Very good."

She reached her arms around him and kissed his cheek.

He hugged her tightly. "Good night, baby," he said, and got to his feet to turn off the light.

"I'm not a baby" came indignantly out of the darkness, then was followed immediately by a gasp of surprise. "Jared! Look!"

He stopped on his way to the door. "Where?"

"Up there!"

He looked up and saw stars twinkling from Libby's border. She'd put something in the paint to make them glitter in the darkness.

"Wow!" Savannah breathed.

"Cool," Jared agreed, smiling over the fanciful touch. "You can wish on one. Do you know about wishing on a star?"

"Yeah." She launched into the first few bars of the tune heard often on the Disney Channel. "It's like magic."

"Yes. Sometimes. Kind of."

"Can I wish for Mommy to come back? And Daddy?"

He wandered back toward the bed, wishing he'd never brought the subject up. She was trying so hard to adjust.

"No," he said firmly but with difficulty as he squatted beside her again and patted her tiny hand. He had to clear his throat. "Sometimes wishing on a star is supposed to make dreams come true, but people who've gone to heaven don't get involved in dreams anymore. You have to wish for things in the future."

"What's the future?"

"Things that haven't happened yet. Things that could happen tomorrow."

"Oh." She was quiet a moment, then she said briskly, "Okay, I know. I'll wish that if Mommy can't come back that Libby could be my mommy."

Oh, good. He'd averted a possible encounter with grief, only to have to confront the impossible.

But he didn't have to tell Savannah it couldn't happen. She was entitled to wish for what she wanted to wish for. He just had to remind her that magic was chancy.

"Sometimes..." he said cautiously, "wishes don't always come true. Sometimes there are other things planned for us that we can't even guess about."

"But Libby *made* the star," she said emphatically, determinedly. Then her small right hand shot out in the darkness to point to the largest star on the wall facing her. It sat just above the central spire of Notre Dame Cathedral. "I'm gonna wish on that one."

That little hand came back to settle on his in which he'd enfolded her left hand. He remained still, his much larger hand sandwiched between her two, energy emanating from her as she made her wish.

She wrapped her arms around him again and kissed his cheek. "Good night," she said again. She sounded lighthearted.

He'd become enough of a parent in the brief week he'd had her to be unwilling to do anything to dilute her happiness.

He hugged her again and left the room.

From his room, he heard Libby's television clearly. She was listening to the Arts and Entertainment Channel, if he wasn't mistaken. Something British.

He frowned as he stood just beside the door that adjoined their rooms. He knew she would not have ignored the child's knock if she'd been awake. Then he remembered how she'd complained about muscle pain when they'd had cocoa in the kitchen. Was she in pain or simply asleep?

He put his hand on the knob, prepared to turn it, then stopped himself. What if she *was* awake and he walked into her room uninvited? As his employee, she'd have a sexual-harassment case against him before he could even explain.

He considered that a moment, then turned the knob. He'd be damned if he'd be held prisoner and be prevented from checking on someone's good health by the possible extremes of political correctness.

He opened the door. All he could see was the top of Libby's head against her pillows. He moved cautiously into the room and said her name quietly, afraid of terrifying her if she was awake.

When there was no response, he moved farther in and judged, by the arm dangling limply off the bed and the absolute stillness of one long and creamy thigh exposed by a parted robe, that she was fast asleep.

He went quietly to turn off the television, then moved back to the bed. He took the blankets she'd kicked to the foot and pulled them gently over her. Her brow pleated, she made a little sound between a whimper and a moan, and he froze where he stood, certain she would open her eyes and scream.

But she did something else entirely. She puckered her lips and strained slightly off the pillow as though she were meeting another pair of lips in her dreams.

He was mesmerized. The pull to respond was almost overwhelming. Thick dark eyelashes lay on pale ivory cheeks, and her mouth, drawn into a tight circle like the center of a flower, was pale pink, the lipstick worn off.

A slender hand fluttered on the pillow near a tangle of sunshine-colored hair.

He leaned halfway toward her, willing to flout societal rules again and take his chances, but the pucker turned suddenly to a smile and she rolled over.

Acutely disappointed—and concerned that he was—he readjusted the blankets again, left the room and pulled the connecting door quietly closed behind him.

Chapter Six

Libby heard the thunder as though in a dream. It rumbled at the edge of her consciousness, quietly ominous. No, not thunder. Please not thunder. She tried to cover her ears, but she couldn't move her hands.

Thunder clapped again, louder this time. She saw the flash of light from behind closed eyelids and heard the loud, resounding crash within just a few seconds. It was coming closer. No.

Again she tried to move, but she couldn't free her arms and something was wrapped around her feet. She tried to force herself awake, but she was helpless.

She braced herself, sure she knew what was coming next.

Light flashed as if a light had been turned on; the thunder exploded directly overhead, mingling with the light, creating the effect of a bombing or a train wreck or some other horrible disaster that involved scorching light and mind-numbing sound.

She finally managed to throw off the blankets, perspiration standing out on her forehead, and saw that she was in darkness.

She breathed a sigh of relief. It had been a dream. Then light flared brightly and thunder crashed simultaneously, growling, deafening, terrifying.

Her heart thumping inside her, she scrambled out of bed and experienced a moment of complete confusion. Where was she? Where in *time* was she? Was this some cosmic realigning of her life? Would this all clear, and she would walk out her door and find herself in colonial America or medieval England? Or ten years into the future to her quiet, lonely life?

Panic fisted in her throat. Somehow the latter seemed like the worst of all the possibilities.

Thunder roared again, over and over, making her feel as though it beat on her directly, personally. A cry in her throat, she stretched both hands ahead of her in the darkness and went forward, looking for a door.

JARED AWOKE with the first clap. An instinct, newly in use but deeply ingrained, sent him flying out of bed and running across the hall to the children's room.

Zachary, who'd awakened shortly after midnight but had gone to sleep immediately after a bottle, slept on, impervious to the noise.

Savannah was burrowed under the blankets, but she, too, was fast asleep.

He stood still as the room filled with light and thunder crashed again, closer this time. He was certain that both children would awake at any moment, terrified by the sound.

But they didn't. Thunder crashed directly overhead, the sound shaking the room, vibrating loudly, until it finally diminished. Neither child stirred.

It was probably against some rule, he thought with a grudging smile, for Zachary to be awake while he himself was awake.

He finally left their door ajar, crossed the hall and went back to his bed.

He was debating the options of finding a book or going downstairs and making a pot of coffee, when the door joining his room with Libby's burst open.

He saw her blond hair like a shadow image in the darkness just before she collided with him. She cried out and he caught her arms to steady her. He felt the perspiration on her, heard the agitated way she drew a breath, and surmised that although the children were sleeping through the storm, their nanny was terrified.

"It's all right," he said quietly. "It's just a thunderstorm."

One of her hands moved up to touch his face. "Who are you?" she asked. She sounded truly frightened, completely disoriented.

"It's Jared," he said, trying to ignore the unsettling effects of her fingertips skimming over his lips. He laughed, primarily to distract himself. "Why? Who were you expecting?"

She stiffened under his hands, then a small laugh that sounded like relief escaped her and she collapsed against him, her arms wrapping around his waist, her head settling on his shoulder. "Jared. Jared. Hi. I thought you were some minuteman or... one of Arthur's knights."

LIGHT BURST around them and thunder ground the silence for a long few seconds.

Libby leaned closer, held tighter, and he closed his arms around her and hovered over her protectively.

He felt curiously as though lightning were flashing in his brain. Every sensory corner of it was lit with sudden sharpness. The floral fragrance of her hair wafted around him; her eyelashes fluttered against his throat; her breasts—the ones he'd dreamed about in blush lace—were now crushed against him and restrained by nothing but the fabric of a robe.

The bare leg that he'd covered with a blanket only hours ago was now bare again and braced against his own bare leg. He was in serious trouble.

"One of Arthur's knights?" he repeated, trying to pull himself away from a dangerous vortex that seemed to be drawing him in. "You mean *King* Arthur? And a knight of the Round Table?"

She wasn't herself yet. The usually competent, fearless nanny who had little compunction about spying on him or telling him she thought he was being unfair to his mother, still clung to him, her face burrowed against him.

"Yes. I thought I might be traveling again," she said with a sigh. "Thank God, I'm not."

"Traveling?" he asked. He remembered that she'd mentioned a minuteman as well as a knight. "You mean . . . time . . . traveling?"

She heard him say the words, but they didn't register for a moment. She was lost in the delicious security created by the warmth of his enveloping arms, the solidity of his body bracing hers.

Then she heard the words again: time traveling. And everything jarred within her. He was simply speculating about what she'd just said, of course. He didn't know that that was how she'd come to him. But she'd come entirely too close to revealing her position.

She put a hand to her head and pretended confusion, finding that it wasn't that difficult. Panic did confuse one.

"I...I was dreaming about...a minuteman and a knight," she said, trying to cover her dangerous slip. "I wasn't sure where I was when I woke up. I'm sorry I woke you."

She drew away from him, thinking she should go back to her room before she betrayed any more. She could ride out the thunderstorm by herself—that was what she'd always had to do in the past...or the future?

But thunder crashed again and she flew back into his arms.

"It's all right," he said gently. "We're safe. It's all right."

"This is so embarrassing," she whispered against his chest. "I'm supposed to be the one who comforts the children at moments like this—and here I am acting like one." She pulled away again abruptly, her eyes wide with new concerns. "The children! Are they...?"

"They're fast asleep." He pulled her back into his arms and rubbed gently up and down her spine. "Just relax. It's your weekend off. You don't have to do anything for anyone but you. And we all have our unresolved fears. There's no need to be embarrassed about them." He held her aside for one moment and reached to the chair beside his bed to pull on the jeans and sweatshirt he'd removed to go to bed. He caught her hand and dragged her with him as he left the room. "Come on. I'll pour you a brandy to relax you."

Libby followed, her heart thudding against her ribs, and this time her reaction had nothing to do with fear of thunder. She was reacting to the knowledge that she'd been wrapped in his arms and he'd been wearing nothing but boxers and a T-shirt.

As gooseflesh rose along her limbs, she decided now was not the time to think about that. Jared seemed to be responding simply out of concern for her, but she felt as though the night—the moment—had taken a dangerous turn.

They paused in the doorway to the children's room and saw that both were indeed fast asleep. He flipped a switch on the intercom to open reception in the kitchen, and led the way downstairs.

Lightning lit the kitchen as they reached it, and Libby put her hands up to cover her ears, anticipating the thunder. Jared held her in one arm and flipped the light switch on with the other hand.

It was several seconds before thunder shook the house. It was loud and reverberating, but not directly overhead.

Jared's dark eyes looked upward as he analyzed the sound. "It's already beginning to move off. We seldom get electrical storms here, and they don't usually last very long."

She was ambivalent about that news. She was delighted that the storm was moving away, but she was less than happy that this idyllic time with Jared would end. His attention was strictly the concern of one human being for another. When she was no longer frightened, he would no longer feel the need to hold her—and she had to admit to herself that she wished things were different.

But they weren't. He wanted *her* children, and she was not about to let him have them. So the possibility that something romantic might develop between them was out of the question.

He took her with him to the cupboard and reached to a top shelf for a squat brown bottle with a canning label on it that read Peach Brandy.

"You make your own?" she asked.

He pulled down two snifters. "Darren does. It's pretty good stuff. This way." Carrying the bottle and the glasses, he headed for the living room. "Watch your step until I get the light on."

She heard glass clink against the top of the coffee table, then the stained-glass lamp near the big chair went on suddenly, a little pool of light jeweling the design of pink roses, green leaves and gold highlights.

He pointed her to the sofa. "Sit down," he said, and went to turn up the thermostat.

She tightened the belt of her robe and sat near the middle of the sofa, careful to make certain her knees were covered.

Jared noticed the care she took with the ends of her robe and snatched up the cotton throw from the chair as he went back to the sofa. He opened it out and dropped it over her lap. He had reasons of his own to make sure her knees were covered.

"Did you have a bad experience in a thunderstorm?" he asked as he settled near her. He left half a cushion between them and turned his attention to pouring brandy.

She was entirely too beautiful in the glowing light of the single lamp. Her golden hair was tumbled and fragrant, her eyes wide, her vulnerability seductive.

Attraction to her was a complexity he intended to ignore. After all, following years of happy bachelorhood he was suddenly the father of two little children, the confidant of a mother wanting to remarry after thirteen years as a widow and move to Puerto Rico and the referee between his brother and the woman he loved, who wanted his brother's baby without having to take him as a husband.

And then there was the truckload of artifacts arriving from the castle in Scotland the day after tomorrow. He had to turn his mind back to business sometime soon, or his new family would starve.

"No," she replied, accepting a snifter from him filled with the honey colored liquid. "Unless you consider being all alone in a thunderstorm traumatic. Thank you."

He leaned an elbow on the back of the sofa and turned toward her. "At what age?"

"Eight."

"What were you doing all alone at eight?" He frowned, half expecting some sad story of parental neglect. Then she smiled in self-deprecation.

"Chasing a rabbit," she said, and took a sip of brandy. She opened her mouth to continue, then she gasped and her eyes filled with water. "Good grief!" she whispered on a strangled note, holding her snifter up to look at it. "Nitro in a glass."

He laughed. "Yeah. It's good stuff. About the rabbit."

She cleared her throat. The fire that had rendered her speechless a moment ago now spread a comforting warmth in her stomach.

"I was visiting my grandmother's dairy farm in Wisconsin that summer because my parents weren't getting along very well." She made a careless gesture with one hand, intended, he guessed, to indicate that it had been a problem for her at the time. "I was supposed to stay in the front yard, but it was a beautiful day and I wandered into the woods in the back after butterflies, then

I spotted a rabbit. Well, he was far less excited to see me and he took off when I got too close. I chased him, certain he'd be delighted with having me as a friend if he would just get to know me, but..." She spread both hands this time in a gesture of defeat.

"By the time it occurred to me that he was probably in some underground burrow and I wasn't going to find him, I was thoroughly lost."

He shook his head at her. "And it began to thunder?" he guessed.

She nodded. "My life at that point had been filled with loud, threatening noises I didn't want to hear. I could hear my parents shouting at each other after I'd gone to bed, my mother sobbing. Anyway..." She sighed. "An afternoon storm blew up and I couldn't find shelter. I saw a few trees get struck by lightning and burst into flames. I was terrified. And the sound of the thunder seemed to vibrate in the woods, and in my little mind it sounded as though it were somehow animate and looking for *me*."

She spoke with the calm detachment of adulthood, but in her eyes, he saw the residual fear of the little girl, the fear that would probably always be with her when it thundered.

He wanted to take her in his arms again, but it wasn't safe. Earlier he'd reacted with the simple need to provide comfort and protection. Now it wouldn't be that simple.

"How long before you were found?" he asked, instead.

"It was after nightfall. My grandmother had gathered the neighbors, and one of them found me. I've often thought about all those people who wandered around in the pouring rain and risked their lives among all those trees to find me."

Thunder rumbled and she looked up at the ceiling, apparently tracking the sound. It was definitely quieter, moving away. She sighed as though relieved. She took another sip of brandy. "Anyway," she went on with a playful grin, "since that day I can't watch Bugs Bunny cartoons, ride in Volkswagen Rabbits or go to Playboy clubs."

"Are your parents still together?"

She sighed. "I guess you could say that. They resolved some things, but they died in an auto accident when I was a junior in high school. I lived with a friend's family my senior year, won a scholarship to the Museum School in Portland and took off on my own."

"I'm sorry," he said, thinking it sad that someone who loved to hover over people and try to iron out the wrinkles in their lives had no family of her own to fuss over. That was probably why she fussed over his to such a degree.

She shrugged. "I'm fine about it." Then she downed the rest of the brandy in one swallow and focused on him. "Is it hard for you to look at Savannah every day," she asked, "and be reminded of her mother?"

He wondered what had brought that subject about. Perhaps the fact that she'd shared a weakness and now expected him to share, too. Or maybe she'd simply downed the brandy too quickly.

"No," he answered honestly. "Savannah's such an individual that you can't help but see her for herself."

She frowned, her gaze unfocused, and nodded as though she could agree with that.

"Isn't there a woman in your life now?" Libby couldn't believe she'd asked that question. She was a little intoxicated, she guessed, on Darren's flame-thrower brandy. This was the middle of the night, anyway, and she was in her robe. They'd dismissed the employer-employee relationship when she'd burst into his room and flown into his arms. "What does she think of your bringing two children into the equation?"

"There isn't anyone serious," he said evenly, "and I like it that way. There's no one to consider but me."

"What about a mother for the children?"

He lifted a shoulder. "That would be ideal, of course, but before I came on the scene, they had no one, so it seems to me that having just a father is better for them than having no one at all."

They *had* had someone. Her. But fate had intervened and she'd lost them. It was difficult to let that remark go. But she did, and pushed herself to her feet. He'd been the epitome of kindness tonight. "Thank you, Jared . . . for the—"

She stopped abruptly as the room began to whirl. Exhaustion combined with the trauma of the storm and the quick consumption of a generous portion of Darren's strong brew to make her feel as if she were boneless.

She began to fold.

Jared stood quickly to catch her and lifted her into his arms.

She put a hand to her head and opened heavy eyelids. "Sorry," she said woozily. "I...don't know what's the matter . . . with me."

That was a sentiment he could echo. He didn't know what was wrong with *him,* either. Holding her in his arms felt very natural, very right. And his mind wandered ahead of its own volition to the possible outcome of taking her upstairs if the situation were different. But it wasn't.

"You probably just drank the brandy too fast." He carried her up the steps without hurry, enjoying the light weight of her in his arms. He could feel the rounded curve of her breast under the fingertips of his left hand, the elegant turn of hip and thigh on his right arm, her warmth against his chest and that ever-present floral scent that enfolded him when she was near. "On top of working so hard yesterday and being frightened awake by the storm, I imagine your body's just had it. Relax."

She wanted to. But her body had other ideas. The brandy may have induced it to succumb to sleep, but the moment Jared lifted her into his arms, it came wide-awake, all its processes pulsing.

She'd looped her arms around his neck instinctively and now she became very conscious of the inside of her wrists against the short, wiry hair at the back of his head, of his stubbly cheek against her forehead.

Earlier, when he'd held her in his arms, she'd been able to put distance between herself and the feelings his embrace engendered. But this time she couldn't. This time she was woozy with brandy and temporarily warm with the glow of his kindness and concern. She forgot for a moment that he stood in the way of her having the children, and knew only that his presence in her life suddenly filled her mental viewing screen.

He was the man she'd seen herself with in her girlish daydreams—tall, strong, kind, determined. Passionate.

That last was only conjecture based on the dark depths of his eyes and the underlying restraint she sensed in his touch. And as he carried her into her room and placed her in the middle of her bed, she wanted more than anything to have it confirmed for her.

When he tried to straighten away from her, she linked her fingers behind his neck.

Jared felt the pressure of her sustained hold and thought she was simply still feeling disoriented, unsure. He took hold of her wrists and tried gently to disengage her hands.

"It's all right," he said softly. "You're back in bed and the storm's going out to sea."

But she didn't free him. He saw her eyes gleam in the darkness. "Thank you," she whispered, "for being so kind." Then she raised her head off the pillow and put her lips to his.

He didn't even consider all the practical cautions. All he knew was that he'd wanted to kiss her for days, and having the opportunity to do it at her instigation was a gift he'd never expected.

He reached a hand under her to cup her head and another to brace her back, and reined himself in to let her maintain the initiative.

She gave him a series of small, taunting kisses, her lips warm and flavored faintly with brandy. Then she parted her lips, dipped her tongue inside his mouth and explored with dainty interest.

He had to suppress the desire to devour her.

He responded gently, remembering that she was slightly under the influence of brandy and the remnants of fear. He circled the inside of her lips with his tongue, kissed and nipped at the small protrusion of her bottom lip, then let her take charge as her tongue probed more deeply and her fingers went into his hair.

She broke the kiss suddenly and wrapped her arms tightly around his neck, saying in a wan whisper, "Oh, Jared. I wish..."

But she broke the wish, also, and gave him one lengthy, final kiss, then dropped her arms from around him.

He continued to hold her, one hand still cupping her head. He looked into her eyes and saw tears brimming there.

"What?" he asked. "What do you wish?" If it was within his power, he would give it to her.

She looked back at him, opened her mouth as though to speak, then closed it again. "Nothing," she said finally, her eyes large and sad. "Thank you for...helping me. Good night."

Recognizing a situation he couldn't force, he stood and tucked her in. "Good night, Libby."

He closed the door between their rooms, did one more check of the children, flipped the intercom back to pick up in his room and climbed into bed. But he didn't expect to close his eyes. There was suddenly too much on his mind.

LIBBY FELT a tear roll down her temple and onto her pillow. She turned her face to the window, looking desperately for a star. But there was none. The electrical storm had moved on, yet rain still fell heavily.

It was a good thing there was no star, she thought. She'd have only made a foolish, futile wish.

She would wish, she thought, almost afraid to let the words form in her brain, that he would share the children with her.

Chapter Seven

Jared and Darren sat side by side on Darren's sofa, feet propped up on a modern oak coffee table while they watched the Redskins cream the Bills. Zachary played happily in Darren's lap with a rattle toy, and Savannah worked intently on the floor with paper, tape, felt-tip pens and adhesive labels.

During a commercial break, Darren carried the baby into the kitchen, and returned with a fresh bag of potato chips. He handed it to Jared, who tore it open and poured the contents into the almost empty bowl on the coffee table.

Savannah pushed up onto her knees and approached the table greedily.

"You've already had enough chips to sink a tanker," Jared cautioned, catching her little wrist when she reached out. "One more handful, okay, and that's it, or you're going to be sick."

"I'm hungry," she said plaintively, dark eyes wide.

He leaned closer to her. "You ate more chips than I did."

She smiled winningly and held the bowl up toward him. "Want some more?"

He opened his mouth to try to explain that that wasn't the point, then decided it was futile. "Just one more handful," he said firmly.

"Okay," she said, and scooped up as much as her tiny hand would hold. She dropped the chips into a smaller bowl Darren had provided her on the floor and went back to her mysterious project. It seemed to involve irregular bands of paper closed into a circle with tape.

"When did you start having trouble with the nanny?" Darren asked. He'd returned to the kitchen and come back with a bottle of Chardonnay. He poured a healthy measure into Jared's glass.

Jared looked at Darren in surprise. His brother wasn't usually able to read his mind. It occurred to him that he must really be transparent if his problems were clear to Darren.

He indulged himself by resisting an admission. "I'm not having trouble with the nanny. She's great with the children."

Darren took a sip of his own wine, then put it aside and, propping his feet on the edge of the coffee table, leaned Zachary against his raised knees.

"I noticed that." Darren angled him a knowing glance. "But I've seen you look at her. You're thinking she'd be good with you, too."

"No, she's meddlesome. I hate meddlesome women."

"Then resign yourself to permanent bachelorhood. They're all meddlesome."

They were quiet for a moment. Darren cheered a pass. Jared couldn't concentrate on the game. He couldn't clear his mind of the memory of Libby in his arms in the cool darkness of her room, of her arms wrapped around his neck, of her voice sounding curiously sad making an abortive wish.

He sighed.

Darren turned to him, his thumbs caught in the baby's fists. "What are you doing here on a Sunday?"

"It's her day off," he replied defensively.

"So, why didn't *she* go out?"

"Because she's painting a border in Savannah's room, and I didn't want to be in her way."

That made no sense. He knew it didn't.

"You mean you ran away from home because she's there." It wasn't a question. Darren seemed convinced he understood the problem.

Jared took a long gulp of wine. "Yeah. I think so. She woke up last night during the thunderstorm, afraid and confused, and I...all I did was hold her." He leaned his head against the back of the sofa and groaned, anguished by his own reactions. "But I felt like I was twelve and dreaming about seducing Laurie Biederman. Remember her?"

Darren nodded, his eyes losing focus as he thought back. "Do I. We could watch her sunbathe one block over through Dad's telescope. That was a chest for the Hall of Fame."

Jared rebuked him with the jab of an elbow. "Watch it. I've got children here."

Darren came out of his thoughts. "Then I'm right. You're lusting after the nanny."

"It's not lust, precisely. It's interest," Jared corrected, trying to analyze what he felt as he spoke. He'd been working on it all night and still couldn't figure it out. "It's wanting to know more, to break the employer-employee prison without... I guess without surrendering the protection of it."

Darren appeared to consider that, then shook his head. "I don't think you can do that. You can't protect yourself from what a woman could mean to you. Her power is insidious."

Jared took another sip of wine and studied his brother sympathetically. "You have it out with Justy the way I told you?"

"Of course not. I may be able to preach this stuff, but I'm not so sure I can practice it."

"Then why am I listening to you?"

"Because you've been eating my food all afternoon and you feel obligated."

"All right. As long as I have a good reason."

"Anyway." Darren lifted the now-sleeping Zachary off his knees and tucked him into the crook of his arm. He stroked the baby's bald head and studied the tiny features in apparent fascination. "You're better at family life than I am. You've usually got the answers to everything. You're already adjusting to being a father."

"One divorce doesn't mean you're unable to have a family life. Nobody's ready to do what it takes to hold a family together when he's nineteen." He smiled blandly. "If you recall, I tried to tell you at the time."

"Oh, shut up. Can't you just tell Libby how you feel?"

"Can you tell Justy?"

Darren sighed. "Then what are you going to do? Allow the chance to go by because you're afraid to let her close enough to hurt you the way Mandy did? That's stupid. Not to mention trite."

"No," Jared replied candidly. "She's not at all like Mandy, and I made my peace with that a long time ago. It's just that there's something...suspicious about her.

Not in a criminal way or anything, but until last night, I'd have sworn she was out to prove me incompetent with the children.''

Darren looked up in surprise. "Why? What would she stand to gain?"

"Got me. If there'd been others challenging me for custody, I'd suspect she'd been planted by them. But the agency sent her, so that doesn't make sense."

"Maybe it's just paranoia on your part because you're attracted to her and you'd rather not be."

"Maybe." He turned to Savannah, who'd been standing beside him and patting his shoulder for attention for the past two minutes. "What is it, baby?"

She made a dramatic face of disapproval. "I'm not a *baby*."

"Right. I'm sorry. What is it, you beautiful young lady?"

Savannah took that praise with a very feminine inclination of her head. She held both hands tightly behind her back with a great show of hiding something, and smiled widely. "I made you a present, Daddy. Guess what it is!"

Daddy. The word hit him with the impact of a punch. He looked back into her bright, sparkling eyes and tried not to alarm her with an overwhelming reaction. But he felt a little weak, very humble and deeply shaken.

"Ah . . . a picture?" he guessed.

"No."

"A paper chain?"

"Nope."

"A necklace of potato chips?"

She giggled. "That's silly. No. Give up?"

Her excitement warmed and pleased him. It was remarkable, he thought, how a child's moods could affect one. "Okay. I give up."

"Ta-da!" She held up a band of paper scribbled with blue. An unidentifiable object with several sharp ends was set off in the middle in bright yellow. "I made you a crown!" she announced, obviously very pleased with herself. "With a star on it so *you* can make a wish."

He remained still while she placed it on his head. He was surprised to discover he wasn't at all embarrassed. Her delight in the gift seemed to override his usual cool.

He turned to Darren, daring him with his eyes to laugh. "How do I look?"

He saw in his brother's eyes that Savannah had charmed him, too. Then Darren met his gaze and there was gentle mockery in it, and acknowledgment of his good fortune.

"Very royal," he said.

"I made you one, too, Uncle Darren!" she announced, reaching to the paper rubble on the floor for another scribbled circlet with the same yellow pattern.

A star, Jared now understood. For wishing on.

Darren leaned carefully over the baby for his coronation. Savannah stood back to admire her work, her baby-toothed grin stretching from ear to ear.

"Thank you," he said solemnly. "I've always wanted to be king."

"No, he's the king," she corrected, pointing to Jared. "You're the prince."

Darren sent him a disparaging glance. "Story of my life. Always second to you."

"Yeah, but I'm a noble despot. I always take care of the little people."

"You're lucky I'm holding a baby."

Savannah settled down to make herself a crown to match, and Jared and Darren focused on the television again in time to see the camera panning a screaming, flag-waving crowd.

"What happened?" Darren demanded.

"No idea," Jared replied. "I was busy with matters of court."

Darren groaned as the announcer explained an interception that everyone would be talking about for days—a play—and a replay—that they'd missed.

He turned to Jared, wry amusement in his eyes. "Did you think it would ever come to this? The two of us watching football on a Sunday afternoon with a baby in my arms and a little girl at your feet?"

He hadn't, and it was beginning to change him. He could feel softness creeping into his emotions where he'd maintained strict security. And he found himself thinking that since he'd opened himself up to the children anyway, what would be the harm in seeing what might develop with Libby?

But he knew it wasn't as simple as that. Placing yourself at a child's mercy was less dangerous that opening yourself up to a woman. And it was generally unlikely that a child would leave you for another father.

He hated problems he couldn't solve.

"No," he answered. "And your crown's crooked."

LIBBY COULD NOT dispel the feeling of impending doom. And she didn't pretend to wonder what supernatural forces were at work to cause it.

It had nothing to do with the cosmos, or the weird kink in time that had sent her back, or any other kind of paranormal activity. It was her own guilty conscience.

All afternoon while she'd finished the border in Savannah's room, she'd thought about what she'd done. She'd lied, she'd pretended to be someone she wasn't and she'd weaseled her way into Jared Ransom's household for the sole purpose of finding a way to wrest the children from him.

She was still firmly convinced that her goal was just—even ordained, judging by the way she'd come back in time. But the end never justified the means.

She marched up and down the driveway in the cold darkness, hoping the biting air would clear her beleaguered brain.

She was going to tell him tonight. He would think she was insane, but she would explain everything from her thirty-fifth birthday party, to the bicycle that landed her in the hospital, to the incredible discovery she'd awakened to, to Jared's misunderstanding when she appeared at his door.

Then she would fall upon his mercy and ask if he would keep her on as nanny so she could be near the children. After that... Last night with all its small but delightful discoveries played over in her mind's eye for the hundredth time that day. She could feel his warm, strong arms holding her; feel his lips nibbling along hers, his fingers in her hair.

Longing so strong it ripped her feelings of guilty conscience aside took center stage. He was a man worth loving, and he had the children she was supposed to have. The answer was obvious.

If he let her stay, she would make him fall in love with her. They would be the family the children needed, and the kind of lovers who became legend.

The loud screech of tires brought her out of her thoughts to sudden awareness. She jumped back as two bright lights stopped inches in front of her. One foot on the edge of a dip in the gravel, she lost her balance and went down with a little scream of surprise.

Jared's heart lurched as he caught sight of Libby in the path of his headlights. He slammed on the brakes, certain he couldn't stop in time, and watched in horror as she fell.

Convinced love had been stolen from him for a second time, he tore out of the car while it rocked to a stop and ran to the still figure on the gravel.

"Libby, God! Libby!" He knelt beside her, vaguely aware that Savannah, strapped in her car seat, was screaming.

Afraid to move Libby, he put a hand to her throat, feeling for a pulse. And as he did that, she groaned, pushed up on an elbow and winced at him.

"Hi," she said, her voice a little faint, as though she'd had the wind knocked out of her. "I didn't see you."

Relief overwhelmed him for a moment, then the residual adrenaline in his body demanded an outlet.

"Oh, I can see why," he said, taking hold of her upper arms and pulling her to her feet. "It's just a two-ton truck with two headlights and two red running lights! What in the hell are you doing in the driveway?"

"I was...getting some exercise," she said, trying to yank out of his grip. She knew she'd frightened him, but she hadn't done it deliberately. She'd been pacing to try to figure out how best to tell him the truth.

"In the dark?" he demanded. "In the driveway?"

A little edgy herself, she shouted back, her arm still pinned in his hand, "Why not? Are there rules about when and where you can get it? I've been working in Savannah's room all day and I wanted some fresh air.''

He held her one more moment, his gaze thunderous, then he freed her arm and shifted his weight. "I almost ran you over," he growled.

She straightened her jacket and tossed her hair. "I'd be happier if you were more pleased about the fact that you didn't."

He glared at her another moment, then turned back to the truck. Through the open door, she could hear Savannah and Zachary screaming. She ran to lend a hand.

He held the screeching baby on his hip and pulled at the buckle on Savannah's car seat.

She reached to take Zachary from him. He resisted for an instant, and she said angrily, "If you tell me it's my day off, I'll hit you."

He freed the baby and she marched off to the house with him. He pulled Savannah from her car seat. He knew she hadn't seen anything but was reacting to the atmosphere of fear that surrounded the moment.

"It's all right," he told her, striding toward the house. "Libby's okay. It's all right."

Libby got coffee going, hot water boiling for cocoa and the baby's bottle warming while Jared built a fire.

He fed the baby while she made Savannah's cocoa, then helped her with a bath. In yellow-footed pajamas, Savannah stood in the middle of her room and admired the completed border. Libby turned off the lights so that the stars would gleam.

"Now I can wish on lots of stars," Savannah said excitedly. "Do you want to make a wish?"

Libby caught her hand and drew her toward the window seat. "I think you have to wish on an outside star if you want the wish to come true."

Savannah frowned at the starless sky. "But where are they?"

"They're there," Libby said. "They're just resting behind the clouds. Do you want to wish for something?"

"I already did. But I wished on that star." She turned to point at the big star near the central spire of Notre Dame on her wall. "Daddy said it's okay."

Daddy. So she did feel secure enough about Jared for him to become "Daddy." Libby was not entirely surprised when that revelation failed to horrify her. As recently as yesterday morning, it would have terrified her, made her feel as though her chances of gaining the children were diminishing.

But now she had a new hope. If she could make the children's father hers, the children would follow.

She ruffled Savannah's hair. "Then it must be okay. Come on. Let's get you into bed."

"Isn't Daddy gonna tuck me in?"

Jared appeared as though on cue, a bright-eyed Zachary on his arm. "You want to trade?" he asked Libby. "I'll put her to bed if you'll wear him out."

"You're being optimistic," she said with a wry smile, taking the baby from him. "But I'll do my best. Good night, Savannah."

"'Night, Libby."

Libby took the baby downstairs to the living room, where the stained-glass lamp bloomed light in a corner of the cozy room. A fire crackled in the fireplace, raying warmth toward the sofa, where she propped the baby up against a wedge of pillows.

Zachary gave her a wide, toothless smile and flailed both arms, delighted with her attention.

"So, what did you do today?" she asked, tucking her legs under her as she curled up beside him. "Did you go to town again? Visit friends? I put in a long day at the top of the ladder, trying to finish your sister's room. Did you notice how good it looks? I'm sorry I frightened you and Savannah and your... dad." It was still a little difficult to say the word, but she knew denying their growing relationship wouldn't make the fact of it disappear. And if she was going to find a way into their lives, she had to know what she was dealing with. "I was just trying to clear my head."

As Jared reached the bottom of the stairs and rounded the corner into the living room, he heard Libby talking to the baby, her tone high and soft. He felt a stab of guilt for having shouted at her—and a strong wave of electric awareness when she heard his approach and smiled at him over the back of the sofa.

"Hi," she said, her voice going down an octave for him. "Savannah asleep?"

He nodded. "The minute her head hit the pillow. Your border in her room is a masterpiece. Even I kept staring at the stars in the dark."

She shrugged. "I had the luminescent paint for a craft project I'd done for the hospital, and it seemed like a good idea. I'm... sorry about frightening you in the driveway."

He shook his head and went to sit beside her. "That was my fault. I came tearing into it, not expecting anyone to be there. No ill effects from the fall?"

"Just a skinned elbow."

"This one?" He caught the arm closest to him and gently pushed her sleeve up. A rough, red scrape covered several square inches of flesh.

"It'll be fine," she said, trying to draw her arm away. "I've washed it, and I'll put something on it when we go to bed. When . . . I . . . go to bed." She guessed nothing would have happened if she hadn't corrected the innocent remark. It was just that it had sounded as though they'd be going to bed together, and because that thought had been on her mind much of the afternoon in the interest of sharing the children with him, she was sure he'd read that into it.

As it was, he seemed to pay no attention, until she corrected herself. Then she saw something ignite in his eyes, and without warning, she was in his lap.

She whispered his name. "Jared!" There was surprise in the sound, but not dismay. She knew he'd heard that note when he smiled.

"I've been thinking about you all day," he said, his lips a mere centimeter from hers. His dark eyes roved her face, and she felt her body's tension begin to melt in the warm comfort of his arms.

"You have?" she asked, a soft quiver in her voice.

"I have." He ran a hand lightly up the thigh of her fleece pants, his gaze holding hers. "I can't get last night out of my mind."

She quirked her lips. "I acted like a child."

"No, you didn't," he corrected gently. "What I remember most is that you kissed me. Do it again, Libby. Now."

It occurred to her to wonder how this could be happening. But he'd lost patience with her hesitation and put his lips to hers.

The kiss began as last night's had, with a gentle edge of exploration, of sharpening interest, of fascination. Then he assumed control, dipping her sideways into his supporting arm and plundering her mouth with possessive purpose.

All her inhibitions and protective instincts were drawn out by the kiss and cast aside. She responded eagerly, fueled by his ardor and the tenderness of his touch.

His hand stroked up her thigh, then over her hip and down to her knee as she curled into him.

She kissed the line of his jaw, the lobe of his ear, his temple. He nipped along her throat, the underside of her chin, then buried his nose in her hair.

The baby gurgled and she lifted her head abruptly, horrified that for a moment he hadn't been uppermost in her mind. He was smiling widely and rattling his ring of plastic keys.

Jared touched an index finger to the tip of his nose. Zachary squealed delightedly.

"He's fine," Jared said, his hand curving Libby's hip as he drew her closer again. "He's within my reach. Kiss me."

She pushed at him halfheartedly, trying to surface from the desire billowing in her to remember that she'd intended to speak to him about how she'd gotten here. And with this sudden ignition between them, the need to do that was growing more and more urgent.

"I . . . have to tell you . . . something," she said as his mouth roved over hers with taunting little kisses.

He groaned and covered her mouth with a deep, lengthy kiss. "We'll talk later."

That was definitely the way she'd prefer it, but as his lips traveled down her throat again and she felt his fingertips at the buttons of her sweater, she forced herself back to the issue.

"Jared, listen . . ." But he'd parted the top few buttons and the touch of his lips against the swell of her breasts made her forget every thought in her head.

His hand had slipped under the back of her sweater, and she felt it splayed between her shoulder blades, warm and strong and artfully seductive as it began to stroke.

Jared felt intoxicated by the depth of her response. She was like silk in his arms, entwining him, enfolding him. Now that he'd distracted her from the silly notion of talking, she was reaching under his shirt.

The first touch of her slender hand against the bare flesh of his abdomen caused his muscles to clench with the exquisite sensation.

He heard himself whisper her name, then she covered the sound with her lips and moved her hands around him to his back. He swung her astride his lap and sat forward to accommodate her. They kissed and stroked and finally drew apart to gasp for breath.

He looked into her eyes. "This would be easier upstairs," he said, kissing her again.

In a hot cloud of need and desire, Libby turned to the baby and saw that he'd dozed off, the keys still in his fingers.

"I'll put him in his crib," he said, nipping at her earlobe, "and meet you in my bed."

There was nothing she wanted more at that moment. She even considered falling in with his plan and telling him afterward how she'd come into his life. Surely after they made love, Jared's reaction to her deceit would be sympathetic and understanding.

But as determined as she was to be Savannah's and Zachary's mother, she couldn't make love with their father without telling him the truth. If he became furious and could not understand what had motivated her, then she would take him to court.

That was a strange thought to entertain, she realized, losing her fragile grip on coherence when she felt his fingers at the fastening of her bra and his lips on her warm flesh.

"Jared, we—" she began on a fragile whisper, but the peal of the doorbell interrupted her.

He raised his head to swear roundly, then slapped lightly at the thigh under his right hand.

"That's what happens," he said with a wry grin, "when you don't seize the moment."

He held her hands to steady her as she climbed off him, then used them to keep her still while he ignored a second peal of the bell and leaned over her to kiss her soundly. "Let's hold on to our momentum. You put Zack to bed and I'll get rid of whoever this is and meet you upstairs."

By the time he reached the door, the bell was pealing continuously. Libby lifted Zachary carefully and turned in the direction of the stairs. But the sound of her friend Sara's anguished voice stopped her.

Her heart rose in her throat and began to pound there.

"Jared Ransom?" Sara asked breathlessly from the porch side of the open door.

"Yes," he replied.

There was a sigh and an exchange of feminine chatter. "Oh, thank God. I'm Sara Perez, and this is Charlene Whitney. We're friends of Libby Madison. *Please* tell us she's with you."

"Yes, she is, but I don't under—"

"What a relief!" That was Charlene's voice. "We were frantic when she disappeared! I mean, we left her on the sofa with strict instructions to follow the doctor's orders and remain quiet! Then we went to her place with dinner and she was gone!"

Libby could not have moved had a lion suddenly appeared to chase her. The jig, so to speak, was up. In her excitement at having Jared mistake her for a nanny, thus providing her with an entrée into the children's lives, she'd completely forgotten that her friends would wonder what had happened to her—that they might even come looking for her. She should have forestalled this moment with a message on Charlene's answering machine when she'd run home that first afternoon to pack a bag.

She put Zachary to her shoulder and patted his back, afraid to turn in the direction of the door. She could feel Jared looking at her, sense the suspicions begin to form in his mind.

"We're her best friends in the whole world." Sara's voice again, then she laughed. "Well, at least in Portland. Can we just see her for a few minutes, please? Just to assure ourselves that she's fine?"

"Of course."

The reply was graciously polite, but Libby heard the quiet temper in it, the suggestion of confused anger.

"Come in."

Libby turned as her friends came across the living room toward her. "Hi!" she said, trying to ignore what this encounter could mean to her future and thinking only that these women had worried about her, taken the time and made the effort literally to hunt her down and check for themselves that she was all right.

She would explain to Jared later. Right now, she had to make her friends welcome.

Sara and Charlene came to wrap their arms around her. She hugged one and then the other in her free arm.

"Hi, guys," she said. "I'm sorry I frightened you. Everything happened so fast that I didn't think about letting you know."

They oohed and aahed over the baby, lowering their voices as he whimpered, then nuzzled into Libby's neck.

"We thought you'd been kidnapped or had gone off the road somewhere!" Sara scolded softly, her anger at Libby's thoughtlessness obviously tempered by relief at seeing her well.

"But what are you doing here?" ever-frank Charlene wanted to know. "Did you come to stake your claim to the children?"

Jared walked toward them, outward facade of civility in place. But Libby could see the storm in his eyes. He'd heard Charlene's question about her claim to the children, and though he couldn't possibly understand precisely what was behind it, she was certain he was getting a grasp of the nature of it. Trickery.

With a polite smile for her friends, he took Zachary from her. "I'll put him to bed," he said, "and make a pot of coffee. Sit down, ladies."

Sara and Charlene literally twittered at his charming manner, but Libby saw the fury in his eyes when he claimed the baby. The gesture was significant. She wondered if she'd ever have the opportunity to hold Zachary again.

But that was for later. He was going to listen to her explanation, and if he was determined to be unreasonable, she would take it from there.

But now she had her friends to consider.

And it wasn't long before she was thinking dryly that with friends like these, one needed no enemies. They didn't know, of course, that she'd tricked her way into Jared's life, so they had no cause to be subtle in their questioning. And they weren't. They interrogated her as Jared came and went with coffee and a freshly thawed cake roll Darren had left in the freezer.

"What did he say when you told him *you* were going to file for adoption until the messenger hit you?"

"Did he invite you here, or did you just come?"

"Were the children glad to see you?"

"Are you trying for a kind of joint custody thing or something?" That question was Sara's.

Then Charlene asked with a roll of her eyes as Jared went to check on Savannah, "Or are you working out a more convenient arrangement?" She flicked a finger at the collar of the sweater Libby had quickly rebuttoned, one button off. "He is one gorgeous daddy. And though you use them so seldom, I'm sure you must have skills in dealing with men as well as child-care skills."

So far, Libby had scarcely had a chance to speak, but now she put in quickly, "I'm the nanny."

"The nanny," Sara and Charlene repeated together rather flatly.

"Well, that's a…a nice arrangement," Sara said with a forced smile.

Charlene eyed her skeptically. "But all you do is take care of the children. They're not yours."

"But she gets to be here," Sara defended, trying to quiet Charlene with a look. "And who knows? You know. Something else could develop." She waggled both eyebrows to suggest the very eventuality that had probably just been squashed by their arrival.

Charlene considered that and smiled. "That's the solution to go for, girl. He's nice as well as gorgeous. How is he with the kids?"

"Wonderful," she replied.

"Well then, this could have a very happy ending after all, couldn't it?"

Jared returned at that moment and took the big chair opposite the sofa. She guessed that he hadn't missed a word of their conversation, though he'd been in and out of the room. The intercom was open in all the rooms for the convenience of hearing the children at all times.

She met his eyes and saw that though he had a smile for her friends, the gentle man of only moments ago was gone. In his place was an injured man—dangerous, possibly even deadly.

No, she thought resignedly. A happy ending did not seem to be in the cards at all.

Chapter Eight

Libby walked her friends down the porch steps into the driveway, where they'd parked Charlene's sporty red Sunbird.

"Take care of yourself," Sara urged motheringly, "and when you get a vacation, call us, and maybe we can all do something together. We can't go to Truffles without you, you know."

Libby felt as though she'd swallowed a cannonball. Dread sat in the pit of her stomach like something weighty and totally indigestible. But she smiled cheerfully as her friends climbed into the car. "Of course I will. I'll write often and call when I can. And the moment I can get to Portland, I'll let you know."

Sara waved madly as Charlene looked over her shoulder to back out, then there was one final tap of the horn and they drove off into the darkness.

Libby wished more than anything that she could just run away into the night and not have to explain herself to Jared. But that would mean she'd have to leave the children behind, and wanting them so desperately was what had hatched this plot to begin with.

And now it was more complicated than that. Now she wanted him, too.

All right. She turned toward the house and squared her shoulders. There had to be a way to make him understand why she'd been less than honest.

His tall figure was silhouetted in the doorway against the living room's light. He seemed to fill it, his stance wide, his hands in his pockets.

She climbed the porch steps. He remained firmly planted in the doorway and she stopped several feet from him, wondering if the challenge to her position in his home had already begun.

He studied her with chilling dispassion. How much his gaze had changed, she thought, from the man who'd devoured her with depthless velvet eyes just an hour ago.

He finally stepped back without a word for her to enter, then closed the door behind her and locked it. Libby went to the fireplace, where the flames were just beginning to die down. She held her hands out to them and felt a meager warmth. She pushed aside the thought of how symbolic it all seemed.

Abruptly, she turned to see Jared standing on the other side of the sofa, his hands on his hips, his weight on his right leg.

"I can explain," she said quietly and with as much dignity as she could muster.

"Oh, good." His voice was cool and mocking. "Start by explaining why your friends think you're a waitress, but you told me you were a nanny."

That was the toughie. She drew a deep breath. "If you'll remember," she began, "I never told you I was a nanny. You presumed the agency had sent me, and I...I let you believe it."

He turned away from her in disgust, took a few paces, then turned back again, anger alive in his eyes.

Somehow she found that a relief. Knowing he was furious was somehow easier to deal with than thinking he was coldly indifferent. Particularly since her feelings were so strong in the matter—in several ways.

"You're not suggesting," he demanded, "that that absolves you of lying to me."

She angled her chin. "I am. You needed a nanny, and I stepped into the role. It's true that I haven't been a nanny before, but can you say I haven't done the job well?"

He couldn't, and that was what fueled his anger. Like any red-blooded male, he hated the thought that he'd been deceived—and more than that, he hated the thought that he hadn't even *suspected* he was being deceived—at least, personally.

He'd made such a point of being vigilant with women since Mandy. He'd told himself he wasn't cowardly enough to try to protect himself from getting hurt again, but simply from the embarrassment of being stupid.

Yet this little blond waitress had managed to make him look precisely that.

"You misrepresented yourself," he accused brutally, "and you lied. There is no way to sugarcoat it, Libby!"

"I love those children!" she shouted at him, the words erupting out of her strong emotion. "And I wanted them!"

That declaration was still echoing in her ears when she realized what a mistake it had been. She'd intended it to justify her deceptive manipulations, but what it did, judging by the turbulence in his eyes, was show him that from the very beginning she'd been working against and not for him.

His gaze narrowed on her. "You *wanted* them," he repeated ominously.

She read the outrage in his eyes and spun back to the fireplace for a moment, trying to collect herself. She had to remain rational. She had to see that *he* remained rational.

He caught her upper arm in a viselike hand and yanked her around. "What do you mean, you *wanted* them. Why? You're not related. Miller told me he'd searched for relatives . . ."

"No, I'm not related." She tried to yank free of him, but he held her in place. Resigned, she began a partial explanation. "I told you I knew them from the hospital."

He raised an eyebrow. "You mean that part was true?"

She sighed wearily. "Do you want to hear this?"

"No, I don't," he replied mercilessly. "I'd like to just toss you out on your pretty little butt and never have to see you again, but I need some answers first."

She had so little leverage in this exchange that she grasped at straws. "You start talking about my pretty little butt, Mr. Ransom," she threatened, "and I may have to bring you up on charges of harassment."

He made a scornful sound. "Really. You must be forgetting that *you* ran into my room in the middle of the night and flung your arms around *me.*"

She stiffened. "That was genuine fear. I wasn't quite awake. Your remark was simply patronizing."

"Allow me that, Miss Madison," he said, imitating her sudden bristling formality. "You lied your way into my household. Where the safety of two little children is concerned, I think any judge would be on my side. Now, do you want to continue to explain, or shall we keep threatening each other?"

"You might want to let me go," she said, a sweep of her eyelashes indicating his grip on her arm, "before bruises form. That might very well sway a judge in my direction."

He considered her a moment, grudgingly decided she was right, then pulled her aside to line her up with the sofa and gave her a gentle but firm backward shove that landed her in the middle of it. "Then sit down and tell me the rest of it while I still have the patience to listen."

She glowered at him. This was what he was like *before* he lost his patience? She opened her mouth to comment on that, then decided against it.

"I fell in love with them, all right?" she said candidly, abandoning all attempts to put it delicately or to work around him so that he saw things her way. That suddenly didn't seem like a possibility. So she may as well go for broke. "They were so sweet and beautiful. They were also very alone and so was I. Mr. Miller had been trying to locate family for four days, when he suggested that I was getting along with them so well, I might consider adopting them."

He sat down in the corner of the sofa nearest the fireplace, his body angled toward her. The lines of his face were rigid and severe, though she thought she saw something flicker in his eyes. Compassion, she wondered, or just the movement of the flames cast against his profile?

"When I arrived in his office," he said, "he told me no one had come forward to take the children."

Her throat tightened painfully when she remembered how close she'd come to having the children to herself. "I was on my way to his office," she said, her voice raspy, "and had an accident. I wasn't hurt severely, but I was unconscious for two days. When I came to, you'd already taken them." She withheld the detail that she'd come back in time with a second chance.

He looked skeptical. "Coincidental timing."

She shrugged a shoulder. "If you think I'm lying, you'll recall that my friends mentioned having left me on the sofa with the doctor's instructions to stay down."

"I remember," he said grudgingly. "But that's when you came to my hotel suite."

She nodded. "Mr. Miller told me you were there."

"And you just happened along at the same time that I was waiting desperately for help from a nanny service."

"Yes." She admitted with a small smirk, "I met the nanny from the agency in the hallway when you sent me home to get my things. I told her I was your secretary and that you'd already filled the position and checked out."

He frowned. "And she believed you?"

Libby met his gaze blandly. "Didn't you?"

He wasn't pleased at being reminded of that. "Why didn't you simply tell me the truth?" he asked.

She slapped both hands on the sofa cushions in exasperation. Why hadn't she, indeed? "Because I'm a part-time waitress with no bank account and very few possessions. It would have been one thing had I been the only one available to adopt the children, but pitted against you—the paragon of education, accomplishment and stock-market successes—I hadn't a prayer. So..." She drew another deep breath and looked boldly into his eyes. "So, I'd just come to see you to try to tell you how much I loved Savannah and Zachary. To see if maybe you were wishing you could unload them on somebody. When you mistook me for the nanny, it came to me in a flash. If I could observe you in action as a father and find fault, I could build up a case for getting the children away from you. Or, failing that, I would be around to take over when you decided that a bachelor adopting two young children was a big mistake. I was pretty sure that one way or the other, I'd come out on top.''

He looked back at her a moment as though he couldn't believe her audacity. Then he asked with quiet arrogance, ''And that's usually where a manipulative woman likes to be, isn't it? On top?''

She replied in the same tone, ''And that's always what the bull male fears most, isn't it? Loss of power and control.''

He wasn't going to argue that issue with her. He'd come very close a little while ago to letting her be wherever she wanted to be as long as she made love to him. And now that rankled him, as well as filled him with profound regret. So he fell back on the real issue.

''You lied to me.''

She accepted that accusation without denial this time. ''I wanted the children. And frankly, that first day, I didn't think you were going to be able to cope.''

Frankly, he'd had several occasions of real doubt himself.

''You lied to my mother and my brother,'' he further accused.

Again she had to accept that she had. ''I do regret that,'' she admitted gravely. ''I like them both. I'm sorry.''

''Just how far were you willing to go?'' he asked coolly. ''Into my arms, then into my bed, aiming unerringly for into my *life?*''

"No." The denial was whispered on a gulp of indignation. Until that moment, she hadn't even guessed he would think that, though as she gave it thought, it seemed like an obvious conclusion after the way she'd reacted to his embrace the night before and the way she'd melted in his arms earlier that night. But her response to him had been honest, the result of feelings she'd harbored for him since the first time she'd seen him.

"Then that was love," he said, his dark eyes as blatantly disbelieving as his tone.

She met the mockery with her own even gaze. "No," she said, staring him down. "It was interest, possibly even fascination. You're wonderful with the children, despite your inexperience, and you were kind to me in a way that made me feel . . . cherished. That'll stop any woman in her tracks and make her want to learn more about the man."

That admission seemed to startle him for a moment, though hardly a muscle twitched in the set lines of his face. Then he stood and paced away from her. She had the most horrible feeling that all her honesty had done was alienate him.

Jared felt a clutch of panic in his chest. He didn't know whether to believe her or not. All his male instincts told him she hadn't been pretending anything, but then, those same instincts hadn't alerted him even once when she'd been convincing him she was a nanny. They couldn't be trusted.

And neither could she—about anything. He turned to face her, looking past the love in her eyes for the children down to the woman who'd lied to him.

"I'm terminating your employment, Libby," he said, relishing the distress he knew this would cause her. His self-satisfaction was deflated the next moment when he saw pain standing in her eyes, darkening them to deep blue. But he made himself go on. "I'd like you to pack and be ready to leave in the morning. I'll hire a car to take you back to Portland."

She held tears at bay through strength of will. "You know I wasn't reacting to you because of the children. I did trick you about being a nanny, but not about caring for you."

He jammed both hands in his pockets. "You'll forgive me if I find that difficult to believe."

She stood, trying not to think about her future draining away. He seemed to find it so easy to hurt her; she wanted to hurt him back.

"I know you find it difficult," she said, "but I don't think it's because of me. I think it's because you never forgave Mandy for loving your friend more than she loved you."

He knew that at some level that was probably true. Because he'd loved them both, he'd suppressed the anger he felt, knowing it shouldn't be directed at them, and therefore had never found an outlet for it. He'd been determined to live around it.

And it had worked until he'd learned about the children—and until the nanny who really wasn't had walked into his life.

"That's none of your concern at this point," he said, his tone mild, though his eyes were not. "And if you ever plan to try the nanny gambit again, you're going to have to get a better grasp on what concerns you about the family and what doesn't. Or you'll find yourself out in the street again."

"My mistake," she admitted, facing him across the coffee table, "I thought when you cared, everything concerned you. Who'll watch the children tomorrow when the truck arrives with your shipment from Scotland if I'm on my way home?''

That would have occurred to him eventually, he was sure. He was definitely into father mode; he just occasionally forgot to be prepared for the details.

"Justine," he replied as though he hadn't had to think about it.

"What about the shop?"

"It's closed on Mondays."

"Oh." The little word was spoken in a fragile tone. Then Libby sighed deeply and nodded. She felt as if the moment were frozen—a notion that didn't seem alien at all to a woman who'd already played with time once.

She tried to sort through the sense of what had happened. She'd been so sure that reclaiming the children was the reason she'd been brought back. And she wanted to storm off to bed right now with the dramatic parting line that she would see Jared in court.

But love for Zachary and Savannah would prevent her from doing that. They were settling in here, Savannah was thinking of Jared as her daddy and Zachary grinned gummily every time Jared came into view. She couldn't rip them away from the security being reestablished in their lives.

And she could never provide them with the comforts they knew in this wonderful house. Undoubtedly with two small children to look after, *her* future would change and she probably wouldn't have the house at Hessler Hills and the Mercedes.

"Well." She couldn't dispel the feeling that God had stopped the Earth in its orbit, given her a giant push backward to where He wanted her to be—and yet with all that divine interference, she'd still managed to fail.

She hated to think about what the consequences were of a defeat that cosmic. She sighed and fixed Jared with a stiffly courteous half smile. "Thank you for the past week," she said, her voice strained. "Good night."

"Libby!" His voice stopped her on the stairs.

She looked over the railing at a foreshortened view of him in which he appeared to be all shoulders, all solemnity in the face turned up to her.

"You'll be compensated," he said, "for using your weekend to paint Savannah's room."

She shook her head at him for so misunderstanding her. "That was intended as a gift to Savannah. Good night."

Jared watched her disappear up the stairway and knew he'd overreacted. Though she had deceived him, she'd done it because she loved the children. Under his indignation at having been tricked, he understood that and had to admit that was easy to forgive.

But suspecting that she'd lied while kissing him and making him wild with wanting her was another matter entirely. It was probably just ego that made him think it had all felt so sincere. And he couldn't risk being made a fool of a second time.

He checked the fire and, satisfied that it was little more than hot coals, pulled the ironwork doors closed. He flipped off the living-room lights and wandered into the kitchen in search of Darren's brandy. Enough of it ought to dispel the image in his brain of Libby's face, big eyed with loss and despair.

LIBBY TOOK the call from Justine while trying to maintain a little haven of peace in the pandemonium that was the rest of the house, the front lawn and most of the way to the workshop. The truck had arrived early, and the two men who'd driven it from Portland unloaded the contents of Savannah's and Zachary's bedrooms first.

"Speak up, please!" Libby pleaded, holding her left hand against her ear to blot out the sounds of male laughter, Savannah's squeals of excitement and Zachary's distressed cries at being ignored.

"I hab de flu! De flu!" a thick, croaky voice said in a pathetic attempt at a shout.

Libby thought she recognized the caller under the strange dialect. "Justy?"

"Yez, yez! I'b sick. Cad you tell Jared I cand watch de kids?"

"Oh, yes. Of course." Libby felt a tiny surge of excitement. She knew it was heartless, in view of how Justy sounded, and probably unwarranted, because given Jared's attitude all it would do was delay the inevitable, but when the cosmos was at work for you it was hard not to have hope. Anything could happen in a day. "Ah...what can I do for you, Justy? Do you need some soup? Some herb tea?"

"Do, I be fide. I'b got bedicine."

"Darren's here, helping Jared unload the truck. I could send him over with..."

"Do! Absolutely dot!" Justy's foggy voice grew high and agitated.

"Okay, okay," Libby shushed her. "Don't upset yourself. Go back to bed and we'll take care of everything here. I'll call you later to see how you're doing."

"I'b sorry."

"It's okay. Go back to bed."

"My beauty shop!" Savannah shrieked in excitement as Libby hung up the phone. "Libby come see! My Curling Katie Beauty Shop is here!" She grabbed the side of Libby's blue wool pants and pulled her with her.

Libby picked the screaming baby up out of his carrier and put him to her shoulder. He quieted almost instantly.

"Hi, Libby!" Darren greeted her cheerfully as he carried in a child-sized pink-and-purple plastic dressing table decorated with pink plastic daisies. "Where'll we put this superduper froufrou thing?"

Savannah led the way upstairs, giggling excitedly. Libby followed and nixed the plan to put it right in the middle of the floor.

"It'll be in your way, sweetie," she cajoled. "How about under the window nearest the bathroom so you'll be close to water and styling gel and stuff like that."

Savannah was agreeable. Libby followed Darren as he placed the table. "I have to give Jared a message from Justy," she said, "and I've tried to use the intercom, but I think there's so much work going on there that he isn't hearing me. Would you mind keeping an eye on Savannah while you bring in the rest of her things? I'll take Zack with me."

"No problem." He straightened the table, and Savannah stood before it and giggled at her reflection in the mirror. Darren took the baby from her. "Let me have him. I need a short break anyway. You grab a few minutes of peace, and I'll entertain these two until you get back." He made faces at the baby, who laughed. Then he caught Libby's arm as she would have left and asked, "What kind of message?"

Libby guessed from Darren's natural behavior this morning that Jared hadn't mentioned having terminated her. So she replied easily, "She was going to watch the kids today, but she had the flu."

Fortunately, he focused on why she couldn't watch the children rather than on why she would have had to. His frown deepened. "She seen a doctor?"

"Um...she said she had medication. So, maybe. She sounded pretty awful."

"Does she need anything?"

"I asked. She sounded pretty adamant that she didn't want to see anybody." At his concerned expression, Libby added lightly, "She probably has a red nose and watery eyes, and her hair hurts too much to comb it. I told her I'd call this afternoon and see how she was doing."

He drew a breath and caught Savannah's hand. "It's probably all her cussedness rupturing or something," he diagnosed. "Poisoning her system. My guess is all our medical breakthroughs haven't developed an antibiotic that strong."

Libby smiled at him as she turned toward the door. "I think they have. It's called Darrencyllin."

LIBBY FOUND Jared carrying one end of a richly carved, high-backed bench to the far side of the workshop. He and the driver put it down, and Jared stood back to admire it. The other man hurried to help his partner, who was trying to extricate a rolled rug from over his shoulder.

The piece Jared studied was so beautiful that for a moment Libby forgot they were enemies.

Apparently so did Jared. He turned to see her staring at it and said amiably, "Wonderful, isn't it? Know what it is?"

"A love seat?" she guessed.

"A hallway settee," he said, dropping to one knee to pull on what looked like simply a decorative panel. But the tug revealed a drawer, and fitted inside the drawer was a banged-up metal pan.

Libby stared at it in wonder. "What is that for?"

"This provided a place to sit and remove your wet or dirty boots without tracking water or mud into the house. A servant would then remove the pan, boots and all, and the gentry never had to deal with the reality of muddy galoshes."

"Wow. Ingenious."

Libby smiled at Jared over the clever and practical solution, and saw that he wasn't smiling at all but was looking into her eyes, his slightly unfocused, yet intent.

Jared had been groping for a solution to the problem of Libby Madison all night and much of that morning. But he couldn't think of one that wouldn't involve his backing down completely, and that prospect was hard to contemplate.

Still, seeing her all pale and windblown this morning in a shade of blue that brought to mind summer sailing, he might have no alternative.

"Yes," he said briskly, pulling himself out of his thoughts. "I'll have Justy make some pretty colored pillows for it, and it should bring in a good price."

"Speaking of Justy," she said, eyeing the floor as though reluctant to tell him what was on her mind. "She called. I tried to get you on the intercom, but I guess you didn't hear me with all the moving noise."

"Yes?"

She tried to appear regretful. "She has the flu." And then because he looked as though he might quarrel with that, as though he suspected she was lying, she added quickly, "She sounded awful. She's all congested. I asked her if she wanted Darren to go over with hot soup or something, but she insists that she doesn't want to see anyone. You can call her if you don't believe me."

He shifted his weight. "Of course I believe you. She complained about not feeling well Friday."

"She said to tell you she was sorry." Then she added magnanimously, schooling her features into sweet servility, "Can you think of anyone you'd like me to call to stay with the children?"

When he hesitated, she put in calmly, as though it didn't matter one way or the other, "Or I can stay until tomorrow morning, if that would be simpler."

He contemplated her a moment. "You're sure that won't be a problem?"

"None at all."

"Then I'd rather you stayed."

"Fine." The quiet answer concealed her exhilaration. He hadn't said it would be easier if she stayed; he'd said he would rather she stayed. A subtle difference, but one she was happy to note. There was a solution here somewhere; she was sure of it. She hurried back to the house feeling a fragile bud of cheer inside her.

When everything had been unloaded and the driver and his partner had left, Darren prepared lunch.

"It isn't fair that you should have to cook," Libby said, trying to lend salad support as he thawed a brown block from the freezer that turned out to be beef-barley soup. "You brought all Savannah's toys in, then you helped with the rest of the delivery."

Darren warmed soup mugs in the oven. "Not a problem. I think I'll save a little of this and take it to Justy on my way home." He tried to make the suggestion sound casual.

Libby made her reply the same. "Good idea. Don't you get tired of cooking?"

"Nope." He took a chunk of French bread out of a built-in bread box with a roll top. "It's been a passion with me ever since Mrs. Morden's home-economics class."

Libby thought back to her own home-ec class and asked with a wince, "You mean the requisite white sauce made you want to be a chef?"

He laughed and lifted the lid off a garlic pot. He made a disgusted sound when he found it empty, then scanned a spice rack for minced garlic. "No. Mrs. Morden was more creative than that. We made toffee bark, cheese enchiladas and scampi that was to die for. I even continued to love cooking when a few self-important members of the football team decided it wasn't cool and locked me in the pantry on a Friday night."

Libby looked at him in concern as she pulled spoons out of the utensil drawer and began to set the table. "When did you get out?"

"Sunday afternoon."

"No! Your mom must have been frantic."

Darren grinned as he forked minced garlic into a cube of butter. "You might say that. Particularly since she'd just had to bail Jared out of jail. He was hanging Willy Goldbeck by his feet off a cliff at North Head."

She couldn't help an answering grin. "Willy Goldbeck, I suppose, was one of the kids who locked you up?"

"Right. Bane of my existence all through school. Jared's very touchy when people don't tell him what he wants to know."

Yes. She knew that.

"I used to resent him a lot when we were kids because he was more athletic than me, better in school, more popular with the other kids. But about the time of the pantry incident, I began to realize that all those things came naturally to him. But except for the usual sibling persecution stuff, he supported and defended me in any and every way. He lent me money to start the restaurant. He waited tables and did dishes for me several times those first few months until I got staff problems ironed out. I even think he hired Justy when she quit the restaurant, so that she wouldn't move away. He brought Mom to stay with him for two months when our father died, and found someone to help her regular clerk in the shop.''

That only confirmed what she was already beginning to recognize. ''Well,'' she said. ''He'll make good father material.''

''The best.''

That was wonderful for Savannah and Zachary, but for her—well . . . damn it.

Chapter Nine

Darren left shortly after lunch and came bursting back into the workshop just before four. He had a khaki raincoat on over his tux and looked as if he'd swallowed plastique and was about to blow.

Jared was examining four timber brackets he was considering keeping for himself, when Darren's index finger suddenly wagged threateningly in his face.

"I don't care if she has bubonic plague!" he roared, pointing that finger in the air, then striding across the workroom as though his pants were on fire. Jared assessed the situation and guessed that maybe they were. A hundred people in his dining room couldn't fluster Darren, but one young woman could.

"You've been to see Justy."

Darren wheeled on his heel and strode back to him, hands in his pockets, eyes hot enough to melt marble. "I have been to see the meanest, sorriest-natured, beastiest woman on the face of this Earth, and if I'm ever—ever!—tempted to put aside my instinctive inclination to keep my distance, to extend the hand of Christian kindness . . ." He picked up a turned oak baluster off the sanding table and extended it toward him. "Hit me with this until I come to my senses."

Jared took it from him and put it down again. "She didn't like the soup?"

Darren raised both hands out to his sides in a gesture of profound exasperation. "She wouldn't even let me in to give it to her! She said she didn't want my soup— she wanted my baby. And if I wasn't willing to give it to her, we didn't have anything to say to each other." Darren fell into a Gothic bishop's chair that was missing the finials on each side. "What is *wrong* with her? What's wrong with everyone? Mom's planning to move to Puerto Rico to get married! You're adopting two little kids! And I'm…" Darren rested his head against the high back. "I'm thinking about giving Justy what she wants."

Jared moved the brackets aside and came around the table to lean a hip on it and frown at his brother. "Darren…do you think you can do that? Make a baby and walk away?"

"No," he replied, without needing time to think. "But I'll lay down a stipulation of my own, and if she's willing to comply, I'll do it for her."

Jared was reluctant to ask. "What stipulation?"

"That we live together through conception and until she delivers."

That sounded like trouble. "Presuming that during that time she'll see that you're nothing like her father, that she loves you after all and that she can't live without you."

Darren nodded approvingly. "Well done. See? You could have a criminal mind, too, if you worked at it."

"You're playing with fire, you know."

"Sure I do. But man needs fire. And it's a critical element in my work. I'm accustomed to dealing with it. Don't worry about me."

"Right." Jared rolled his eyes. "I foresee a weekend in a high-school pantry—metaphorically speaking."

Darren grinned. "Come on. Have faith." Then he sobered again and linked his hands across his stomach. "What's with Libby today?"

Jared felt something inside him start in reaction. He was going quietly crazy where she was concerned. "Why? What do you mean?"

Darren seemed to be measuring his expression. "I don't know," he finally replied. "She's behaving a little differently. Despite her energy, she usually seems so serene. But today she's...I don't know. A little nervous. Superficially cheerful, but with an undercurrent of some emotional...something that seems serious. Did you quarrel? Is that why Justy was supposed to watch the kids today?"

Jared straightened away from the table, picked up the balusters and carried them across the room to a crate where he'd stored others. He heard Darren follow him.

"We decided it wasn't working out after all," he said matter-of-factly, hoping to turn off his brother's curiosity. He should have known better.

"Don't lie to me. You fired her? Will you forget those damn things and explain this to me?"

Darren caught his arm and yanked him upright. Jared regretted the years he'd sparred with the puny kid to help him develop muscle.

"Remember that I told you there was something about her that made me suspicious?"

"Yeah."

He related the events of the previous evening, highlighting Libby's friends' visit and skipping over the embraces he and Libby had shared on the sofa before they'd arrived.

Darren digested that, then followed him back to the sanding table. "So, she lied. But it was because she loved the children. Doesn't that excuse it somewhat?"

"It's still a lie."

He tried to look implacable to ward off more questions, but Darren, apparently having come to peace with what he intended to do with his own life, seemed determined to bring him to the same enlightenment.

"It's the fact that you thought she was falling in love with you, but now you think that was all an act for her to be able to stay with the kids. Same elements as the problem with Mandy. That last month, you thought her love was all for you, and she was seeing Frank on the side."

Jared heaved a long-suffering sigh. "I—am—over—Mandy."

"Horsesh—" Darren's commentary was interrupted by the buzzer on the intercom.

Jared went to the switch. "Yeah?" he asked.

Libby's disembodied voice said, "John Miller is here, Jared. He'd like to see you."

That surprised him. He thought they'd settled everything to get the adoption under way. Obviously, there was some detail they'd missed.

"I'll be right there," he replied.

He went across the room to the sink and washed his hands. "Frank and Mandy's lawyer is here," he said over his shoulder to Darren, standing in the middle of the room. "Sorry to cut your analysis short."

"No problem," Darren said. "I've already diagnosed you."

Jared, drying his hands on a shop towel, went toward him. "Lay it on me."

"You're a paranoid man in love, suffering from a fraidy phobia and a tendency to tediousness."

Jared walked past him to the door. "Thank you. I like you, too."

Darren followed him. "I didn't say I didn't like you. I said you're tedious. And scared!" He shouted the last as Jared began to lope toward the house.

JOHN MILLER placed his briefcase on the coffee table next to Zachary's carrier. The baby inside reacted with a broad smile and the flailing of his ring of plastic keys when the attorney leaned over him and smiled.

"He looks wonderful," Miller said, letting the baby take hold of his index finger. He looked at Libby, who had Savannah clinging to her skirt. "And how are you, Savannah?"

"You remember Mr. Miller?" Libby asked her. Savannah had several of the pieces from her beauty shop clutched in her arms, waiting for a hapless victim. "He saw you a few times in the hospital."

Savannah studied him. "I'm not sick now."

"No," he agreed. "You look very beautiful."

"Please sit down, Mr. Miller." Libby gestured to the sofa behind him and took the big chair opposite, Savannah leaning against the arm.

Miller did, and said in renewed astonishment, "I know I said this when you answered the door, but what a surprise it is to find you here, Libby. Though this is a convenient arrangement, I must say. As the children's nanny, you can help raise them without having to be responsible for their support, their education, all those details that would have been so hard for you without Mr. Ransom in the picture."

Libby thought it was very much to Miller's credit that there was nothing in his tone or manner to suggest that any other arrangement had occurred to him. He'd taken her explanation that she'd been hired on as the children's nanny with apparent personal pleasure in that outcome.

"I'm delighted. I've thought about you often since the day you got out of the hospital and called me. I was afraid that you'd be out in the cold where the children were concerned, but good for you. You took charge of your own destiny. I'm proud of you. And happy for you."

Libby accepted his sincere praise without revealing the pain it caused her. She'd taken charge of her own destiny, all right. She'd screwed it up. She didn't bother trying to explain that it looked as though she'd be gone tomorrow. He seemed so pleased with how he thought things had turned out, and she was pleased to live the fantasy for whatever time was allowed her.

"Thank you, Mr. Miller."

He opened his briefcase, shuffled a few papers, then closed it. He cleared his throat and sat back.

He looked nervous, Libby thought. But before she could analyze why that could be, the front door opened. Savannah shot toward it.

"Daddy! I want to curl your hair!" Savannah greeted Jared at the door with a plastic make-believe blow-dryer in one hand and a large purple hair clip in the other.

He lifted her onto his hip, warmed by her bright-eyed excitement. She pressed the clip to reveal lethal-looking teeth and stretched up to place it in his hair. He knew he was devoted to his new role as father when he didn't shrink from wearing the insultingly feminine thing.

But Libby stopped her before she could decorate him with it. She took the child and the clip from him. "Daddy wants to talk to Mr. Miller now, Savannah. Come on. We'll go make some coffee." She smiled worriedly at him. "I'll be right back for Zachary."

He noted the carrier on the coffee table. "I'll keep an eye on him."

He wondered about her concerned expression as he strode into the living room.

Miller stood to shake his hand. "Good to see you, Mr. Ransom."

Despite the smile, there was a reluctance in the man, a nervousness Jared didn't like. But a smile lightened the look suddenly.

"It was a nice surprise to find Libby Madison here," Miller said, sitting down. Jared took the tall chair by the fireplace. "She wanted the children so much. She'd even set up a meeting with me to discuss adoption just before you got back in the country. But she had the accident and never made it."

So that had been true. He was both pleased and unhappy to learn that. It proved that her explanation was genuine, but that only created problems for him.

Yet it didn't touch the matter of her having preyed upon his affections in the interest of working her way more deeply into the children's lives.

"It's very enlightened of both of you to have worked out such an amicable arrangement so that she can also take a hand in the children's development."

Enlightened. That was a word he wouldn't have thought to attach to their situation.

Jared simply smiled. "We're coping well," he said, then asked directly, "what brings you to Cranberry Harbor?"

Miller sighed as though reluctant to admit the reason for his visit.

Jared braced himself for bad news, although he couldn't imagine what it could be. Except that it had to relate to his adoption of the children.

"Mandy's sister has appeared," he said in a rush, as if eager to get it out. "And she wants custody of Savannah and Zachary."

Jared felt a cold, dragging dread, and right alongside it a hot, blind anger. He fought to suppress both so that he could think clearly. He struggled to remember what Mandy had told him about her sister when they'd been going together.

"She left the family when Mandy was nine. She joined a cult or something. She was sixteen or seventeen."

Miller nodded. "Yes. Her Search Period, she calls it. Well, it seems that her search for personal fulfillment led her to Fiji and marriage to Jeffrey Donner, now Lord Barmont, a member of the English peerage. They have an estate outside of London, one in Kent, and he's on the boards of several international corporations."

Jared swore, about to abandon his grasp on reason and succumb to the dread and fury trying to overtake him. He'd had the children such a short time, but already he had no idea what he'd do without them. He struggled to hold on.

"And never in all that time tried to make contact with Mandy?"

Miller inclined his head, accepting his disbelief. "I know. Seems unlikely. But she says she knew she'd abdicated any hold she'd had on her family and felt it better simply to stay away."

"And what, in God's name, makes her think that reveals her as the woman who should raise her niece and nephew? Her history is abandonment and complete loss of contact."

"I agree. I'm on your side."

"You couldn't even locate her when you were searching for family. How did she find out about Frank and Mandy?"

"Her husband subscribes to the *New York Times* because of his business connections. Frank's and Mandy's obituaries were in it along with a short article because of Frank's restoration work on the Met."

That was eerily coincidental enough to be true. Anger was flickering. Dread was growing.

"So, how serious a threat are they to me?"

Miller sighed. "I've been trying to evaluate that, and I'm not sure. The biggest advantages she has, I would say, besides a rather staggering wealth, is that she has a husband. The children would have two parents. She's also a blood relation."

Oh, God. "But I'm Savannah's godfather."

"Technically, that's a provision to guide a child's spiritual development, not the physical person. I don't want to encourage panic, but I think we definitely need a strategy, particularly since there was no will. I've heard from the Donners' attorney, and he has a court date for the Friday before Thanksgiving."

Jared tried to put a date on that.

"Nine days away," Miller clarified for him. "And you have a visit from your caseworker the Tuesday before."

Jared groaned.

"Precisely," Miller said. Then he grinned thinly. "A wife would help you a lot. You weren't planning a stroll down the aisle in the foreseeable future, were you?"

"We found cookies from Uncle Darren!" Savannah preceded Libby into the room, skipping as she carried a plate of cookies. She came straight to Jared. "Mr. Miller gets one first 'cause he's guessing."

"Because he's the guest," Libby amended quietly.

Jared watched as she placed a tray on the coffee table that bore two bone-china cups and saucers in a shamrock pattern he never used, and the sugar and creamer that matched. His mother had bought him the tea set at an auction because she said the green matched his kitchen.

He turned Savannah around and indicated Miller. "All right. Go offer him one."

She complied, and he watched her grave courtesy as she held out the plate, told him the ones with the "white stuff in the middle" were the best, then plopped down beside him to test them out herself, little legs sticking straight out in front of her.

Libby held out a hand to her. "This is a private conversation, sweetie. Come on back to the kitchen with me. I saved you some cookies."

Savannah went along with a minimum amount of grumbling.

"You've done well," Miller praised, taking up a cup. "The day we picked her and Zachary up at the hospital I wasn't sure how well this was going to work. She was so quiet and withdrawn."

Jared nodded, remembering the terror of his first day alone with the children, of that afternoon before Libby arrived.

"Savannah relaxed the moment she saw Libby," he said, almost to himself. "It helped a lot that they already knew her. She got Savannah out from under the bed and..."

"*Under* the bed?"

Jared ignored the puzzled question because his mind had suddenly become distracted by a thought almost too bizarre to contemplate.

If marriage on its own would help his cause, then certainly marriage to a woman with a degree in education who understood children well enough to have a publisher interested in her book should give him an added edge.

It didn't matter, for the moment, that she'd deceived him and used him for her own ends. All that mattered was that she was excellent mother material. And therefore excellent wife material.

He felt as though he'd been given a noogie by the hand of providence. Marriage could be the answer. Marriage to Libby.

"Can you stay for dinner, John?" Jared asked, reaching to the table for his coffee. "I think I have a plan if you have the time to help us work it out."

Miller looked first surprised, then pleased. "Of course. Just let me call my wife and tell her not to expect me."

"MARRIED TO YOU?" Libby glanced up at Jared in haughty disbelief as she sprinkled uncooked rice over chicken breasts in an oblong pan. "No."

Jared leaned against the counter and folded his arms, refusing to be rattled by what he was sure was a calculated attempt to make him sweat.

"I'll make it worth your while," he bargained, watching her walk to the microwave. She reached into it with hotpads to extricate a plastic container filled with a fragrant murky brown substance.

She gave him a bland smile as she passed him on her way back to the pan. "Bill Gates doesn't have enough money to make marrying you worth my while."

He nodded with grim acceptance. "Go ahead. Take your shots. I can stand up to it."

She poured the brown stuff over the chicken and the rice. "That's it. Would you either move or hand me the foil, please?"

He studied the concoction in the pan with concern. "What are you making?"

"Chicken mushroom rice bake, okay?" she said with impatience, physically pushing him aside and reaching into a drawer for the roll of foil. "I'm the cooking-with-soups queen at home because I'm just not brilliant in the kitchen, but fortunately we're dealing with Darren's gourmet soup here and not the contents of a can, so it should be palatable. If you're going to spring guests on me at the last minute, that's what you have to expect."

He grinned. "That sounded very wifely."

She ripped off a piece of foil with a fervent yank that made him suspect she wasn't as disassociated from his dilemma as she would have him believe. She covered the pan with it, pressed down the corners.

He opened the oven door for her and she placed the pan inside, ignoring his remark. "You're sure Mr. Miller is all right out there with the children?"

"I'm sure." He moved to place himself directly in her path. "Zachary fell asleep, and John's a lawyer. He ought to be able to handle a discussion with Savannah."

She set the oven timer and turned away from the stove, to find herself hemmed into a corner by the oven, the counter and Jared's formidable body. Her nerve endings jangled, heat filled her cheeks and energy churned inside her like heated molecules. She didn't know how long she could keep up this pretended resistance. Her intention had been to make him suffer, but the reverse seemed to be happening.

It would have been such a relief to throw herself at him, tell him she'd do whatever was necessary to help him keep the children. But this was a golden opportunity. It was probably even the very fate that had flung her back in time stepping in to see that she accomplished what she'd been sent back to do. She didn't want to blow it by giving Jared all the advantages.

He was so close that she felt heat emanating from his body; that she could see shards of gold in the depths of his brown eyes; that her fingers itched to touch the subtle shadow of beard along his jaw, to trace the line of his lip with a fingertip.

To hold herself together, she baited him. "Jared, why would noble you want to marry tricky me?"

He knew precisely what she was doing; she could see that in his eyes. But he rested his hands on his hips and replied patiently, "I explained all that. It'll give me an edge against Mandy's sister in court. She's a blood relative and I'm just a friend of the family. And even though it was Frank and Mandy's wish that I take the children, their instructions were never made legal. They're going to court a week from Friday."

"And you'd get more points for having a wife."

"Yes. Particularly one with a degree in education."

So. He wasn't even going to pretend that *she* held any personal appeal apart from the child-rearing nature of her sex and the status-raising nature of her degree. All right. It was time to move in.

"You're telling me you're willing to *use* me to get the children?" she asked quite civilly.

He saw that he was giving her a weapon. He had no other choice. "Yes. That's what I'm telling you."

"I see. Yet when *I* used *you* to stay near the children, you found that reprehensible."

He stayed with it. "Yes."

She folded her arms. Her elbow grazed his chest through his flannel shirt. Sensation shot around inside him like a ricochet.

"Is there a double standard at work here?" she asked.

"What's at work here," he replied evenly, "is a determination to keep the children. Without you on my side, I'm not sure I have a prayer. And if I lose them, so do you."

He saw that truth register in her eyes. She turned to look at the window, a pleat between her eyebrows. Then she turned back to him. "What kind of a marriage are you talking about?"

He knew that was a loaded question. He put it back on her. "What kind of a marriage do you want?"

She looked up into his eyes. He squared his stance, ready to take a hit.

"I want a real one," she said, "and if you're keeping John Miller around to have him draw up a contract, I want that spelled out in it."

This was both as bad as things could get and better than he'd hoped. He lifted her onto the counter so that they could face each other evenly. "Define 'real.'"

Her hands lingered on his forearms where she'd taken hold for balance. Then she pulled them away and joined them in her lap. She put on a firm expression. "For me, it means that I want to be treated by you like the children's mother rather than the nanny, and if custody is decided in your favor, I want to remain your wife until both children are grown and on their own."

He couldn't even crystallize a thought that expressed what he felt when he heard that. He couldn't even decide if what he felt was happiness or pain. Or if a state of painful happiness could exist.

"And if I lose?"

"We won't need each other any more," she said gravely. "I'll give you a divorce."

Talk about a win-lose situation. If he got the children, he kept them and her. If he lost them, he lost everything. Well. He'd already been through that once. He supposed he could survive it again.

"All right," he said. He planted his hands on the countertop on either side of her. He needed a little leverage here, something to make her feel as vulnerable as he'd made himself. "But before we sign on the dotted line, I have a point I'd like included."

Her eyes went over his face a little warily, but she nodded. "That seems fair."

"I want us to share my bed," he said directly, "and I don't want to have to wait until we know the judge's decision. There'll be a caseworker coming Tuesday, and her recommendations will count. I want you to look like a loved woman."

Libby lost all wariness in the face of such audacity. She stared at him for a moment. He stared back. "You really think you're capable," she asked in astonishment, "of making such expert love to me that it'll show in my eyes?"

He ran both hands gently up her thighs and grinned. "Absolutely."

She felt the feminine heart of her grow warm and liquid. Unconsciously she tightened one ankle around the other. But this was a war of wills and hers was as strong as his.

"You have my word," she promised, putting her hands to his face, delighting in the flash of surprise she saw in his eyes when she combed her fingertips into his hair and leaned closer. "Just please don't do anything tacky like be specific about frequency." She nipped at his bottom lip. "If you're that good, we don't need it spelled out in the contract."

Then she kissed him mercilessly, her upper body stretched against him, her tongue dipping into his mouth. She put into it all the hopes and dreams she'd entertained for the four of them before he'd found her out. This was her second chance, and it wasn't going to fail through any fault of hers.

She felt herself lifted against him and off the counter and wrapped her legs around his hips instinctively. His hands supported her bottom and she felt their strength and warmth through the soft wool of her pants. The erotic thrill was instant and shockingly total.

She'd thought she had him, that she'd managed to wrest control with this kiss, but he'd taken it back. She was dependent upon his body for support now that he'd stepped back from the counter.

She couldn't quite draw out of the cocoon in which his kiss enveloped her to censure him for it. It occurred to her that—for however long it lasted—this was going to be some marriage.

"Don't you dare drop me," she whispered against his mouth, tightening her arms and her legs around him.

He firmed his grip on her backside, a movement that raised a conflagration in her.

"Not a chance," he said, and opened his mouth over hers.

Chapter Ten

"I now pronounce you man and wife," the short, bespectacled priest announced with a beaming smile. "What God has joined together, let no man put asunder."

The little rustic white clapboard church that had graced the far side of the peninsula since the end of the nineteenth century rocked with a thunderous, joyful recessional played on the old organ by one of the local ladies.

Darren, Jared's best man, and Justine, serving as Libby's maid of honor, preceded the bridal couple down the aisle.

Carlie blew kisses from the front pew, where she held Zachary, who was wearing a tiny suit and tie for the occasion. Savannah clung to the hand of Julio Ruiz, Carlie's Puerto Rican fiancé. The dogs, mercifully, had been boarded in Seattle.

I like Julio, Libby thought, ensnared in a kind of beaded web somewhere between dream and reality. It was so much easier to think of anything else but what she'd done, and what could ultimately result. If Jared lost the children, she would be alone again, but it would be harder this go-around now that she'd spent time with him and the children, now that she knew his family.

She dismissed that thought by concentrating on Julio as they passed the family pew on their way to the door. He was just a few inches taller than Carlie, romantically swarthy and winningly charming, with a wide smile, a warm and lively sense of humor and a tenderness when dealing with Jared's mother that had won Libby over the night before when they'd arrived for the wedding. He'd sung the children to sleep in the husky, romantic baritone that had once spread his fame far beyond the island of his boyhood.

They'd had a long evening of eating and talking, and it would have been obvious to someone blindfolded that Julio adored Carlie and that he would make her happy.

"I like Julio," she whispered to Jared as they stopped at the door, confronted by a sheet of rain outside.

"You're supposed to be thinking about liking *me*," Jared returned, pulling her back from the opening. "Hold on. I think Darren's prepared for this."

"Never fear! The best man is here!" Darren thrust a closed umbrella between them from behind, then flipped the power opening with his thumb. It unfolded before them like a protective shield. "To the rectory. We have to sign the book and your certificate."

Jared took the umbrella, wrapped an arm around Libby and ran with her to the side door of the rectory. He tried it and found it locked.

He held Libby to him as rain fell thunderously against the thin dome that protected them.

They could see Darren and Justy in the church doorway in earnest conversation with the priest.

"Warm enough?" Jared asked her, gently rubbing her upper arm.

She could think of nowhere she would rather be at that moment. Since the decision had been made to marry just four days ago, it was as though each of them had abandoned all suspicions and grudges in the interest of their alliance. And miraculously, an ease had developed between them that made her believe she'd finally found what she'd been sent back for. Not just the children, but Jared and the children—the four of them a family.

"Yes, I'm fine," she replied, her voice a little thready. Her mind was running ahead to what the night would be like.

She saw his gaze read that thought in her eyes, and he smiled, the gesture a paradoxical combination of arrogance and tenderness that was uniquely male.

Darren and Justy ran toward them under another umbrella, Carlie and Julio and the baby under another and the priest and Savannah under still another, Savannah talking a mile a minute.

Jared groaned as they watched them approach. "I wonder what she's telling him," he murmured.

Libby grinned ruefully. "She's probably asking him if she can curl his hair."

"I HAVE A SURPRISE for you," Carlie said. They were partying at the King's Ransom in the early afternoon. Darren had brought in his chef and a skeletal crew to serve them.

Libby had to tear herself away from the magnificent view of the storm over Willapa Bay. Darren's restaurant stood in wild grass on the banks of the bay, a wall of windows looking out on turbulent gray waters. The decor was a cut above nautical, the furnishings and appointments reminiscent of those on a yacht. Everything was mahogany, leather and brass, and white linen stretched everywhere she looked.

"Mom, you make me nervous when you say that." Jared put an arm around her and squeezed her to him.

She sent him a reproving look from under the narrow brim of her flat-crowned red hat. "I meant that Julio and I have booked you a room for tonight at a little B-and-B at the end of the peninsula. We'll stay with Zachary and Savannah. I know, I know." She raised a hand to stem any protest. "You explained very calmly that the move is a strategic one so you can keep the children, but even a convenient marriage can benefit from good sex."

Darren, who'd been about to approach them, heard his mother's last remark and did an about-face. Or tried to. Jared grabbed him by the coat sleeve. "If I have to be lectured," he said, "so do you. Did you know that even a convenient marriage can benefit from good sex?"

Darren cleared his throat and seemed to think about it. "Well, you know, it's hard to think of anything that wouldn't benefit from good sex. Or anyone."

His mother punched his arm. "It's best for married people, because the intimacy it produces when your lives are already promised is a magic that works for you your whole life."

Libby saw Darren's glance slant to Justy, who'd come up beside him—Justy, who wanted his baby but didn't want to marry him. She pretended interest in the bouquet of Stargazer lilies she carried.

Jared and Libby were shooed away early in the afternoon. News of their overnight absence was greeted by Savannah with a pout. Her eyes brimmed with tears.

Jared held her on his hip under the umbrella. "We're going to be home tomorrow in time for dinner. And tonight, Grandma and Julio are going to rent movies and make popcorn and you can stay up as late as you want."

"I want to come with you," she said plaintively. Just when Libby was about to cave in and plead with Jared that they take her with them, the child added with a soulful sigh, "But I know I can't 'cause it's your honeymoon."

Jared and Libby exchanged a smiling glance. "You know what a honeymoon is?" Jared asked her.

"It's a trip mommies and daddies take. Grandma told me."

"We'll bring you back a present," Libby promised, desperate to get a smile. She didn't get it, but did see a gleam of avarice followed by a nod of resignation.

Jared and Libby took turns holding Zachary, then handed him back to Carlic, hugged everyone and ran together under the umbrella to the car.

LIBBY BOUNCED on the bed, trying desperately to behave in a fearless and sophisticated manner. She sank into inches of quilt and a genuine down mattress "Uhoh. I hope you don't have a bad back. This is going to be like sleeping on marshmallows."

Jared put their two small bags in the bottom of the open closet and looked around the room. He'd taken in at a glance that it was an odd but somehow comfortable confusion of federal furnishings, country linens and used-brick fireplace. But his brain had quickly accepted and dismissed the room and focused instead on the sudden, roiling tension in it—and in his companion. Or rather, his wife. That was a sobering thought.

"No back problems," he assured her. "You?"

"No."

He went to the bed and gazed down on her, thinking that she looked about to run. "Any...other problems?"

She sat up briskly. She'd kicked off her shoes and wore brown woolen pants and a soft gold sweater.

"Yes, actually. Well, they're not problems for me, but they present some for you. In all the rush to get married, I never did get a chance to tell you that I have a few habits you might not like."

He went to sit on the foot of the bed. "I already knew that. You're meddlesome, sneaky and distracting."

She opened her mouth to object to his brutal assessment of her, then hesitated over the last adjective. "Distracting?"

"Yes." He stretched out to lean on an elbow. "I'd be furious at you for something, then I'd remember how your hair looks under the kitchen light, how dark your eyes get when you're angry."

Her nervousness seemed to slip a little.

"You did?" she asked softly.

Before the expression in her eyes could distract him again, he smiled. "But I didn't mean to interrupt your confession. Go ahead. What kind of problems are you going to cause me?"

Libby needed a minute to think. So he'd longed for her just as she'd longed for him. That was comforting.

"I love garlic," she admitted, trying to resume that air of nonchalance, but not quite succeeding. "I like to watch TV in the middle of the night, and I have a passion for Alabama. So there you have it."

"Alabama the state?"

"Alabama the singing group. I mention that only because I saw a lot of Springsteen in your CD collection."

He made a careless gesture with his free hand. "I like spicy food, too, and I'll listen to any kind of music but that stuff from the big band era. And coping with the midnight TV would depend on what you were watching."

"QVC."

"That could get you moved to the sofa. Or back into your old room."

She heaved an exaggerated sigh. "I have intermittent insomnia, and nothing's quite as good for it as seeing all the things I can't afford, even at those prices. I finally go to sleep in self-defense."

He pushed himself to one knee then stood. "Insomnia at your age?"

"I guess when you don't have someone to talk things over with, you worry about them a little more. And I was too busy to worry during the day, so I did most of it in the middle of the night."

He nodded commiseratingly, then tweaked her big toe. "Well, now you can elbow me awake and dump it on me."

That thought warmed her until she remembered that she would be able to do that only for an undetermined period.

He started for the bathroom. "I'm going to take a show—"

He was interrupted by a rap on the door. He reversed directions and went to open it. The elegant older woman whose hospitality they enjoyed handed him a giant basket and a bottle of champagne. "These were just delivered for you," she said.

Libby sat up as he brought the basket to the bed. Pearlescent cellophane within the basket enclosed an enormous array of goodies: a tin of pâté, a small box of crackers, fancy cookies and candies, nuts and a pair of glasses to contain the champagne.

Attached to the basket was a note that read: "Only down side to B-and-Bs is no room service! Eat up—and do with the pâté whatever you're inspired to do. Love, Darren and Justy."

"Darren *and* Justy?" she asked. "You mean they did something together that didn't result in one of them being dead?"

So, she was choosing to ignore the pâté crack. That was probably wise, but something had to lighten her up.

He slipped the glasses out from the paper and reached for his pocketknife and its corkscrew attachment. "Yep. And now that we're married, I guess I can tell you that they'll be doing something else pretty significant together, too."

Her eyes widened as she held the bottle while he worked on the cork. "You don't mean . . . a baby?"

"I do."

"Is that wise?"

"It's not my call." The cork was removed with a satisfying pop, and Libby held the glasses up as he poured. "But we're supposed to be concentrating on us today, not them." He recorked the bottle and carried it and the basket to a small table across the room while she held the bubbling glasses.

He came back to take his from her. He tipped the rim of his glass against hers. "To us," he said.

She drank to them, then offered another toast. "And to defeating Lady Barmont."

He drank to that, then put his glass aside and concentrated on building a fire. Beyond the window, the stormy day had turned to stormy dusk, and rain still fell against the roof and windows with a vengeance.

Libby lit a column candle on the small table, then closed the flowered draperies against the harsh weather. Jared's fire began to crackle and catch and the room took on a shadowy coziness that prevailed over the outside threat.

He stood and brushed his hands on his jeans. He turned to find that Libby had poured more champagne and offered him his glass.

"Why, Mrs. Ransom," he teased, "is this a seduction?"

As the atmosphere grew warmer and more intimate, she found the fearless sophistication more and more difficult to hold on to. But she tried. "Why, Mr. Ransom," she replied with an even gaze, "I thought that was a given."

He wasn't sure he liked the sound of that. "You mean, your seduction of me or mine of you?"

"Well...I don't know. I thought we were just after the...the result."

No. He didn't like the sound of that at all. He took her glass from her and put it on the table with his. Then he pulled her down with him so that they sat facing each other on the carpet before the fire.

"We *are* after the result," he said. "We have to look as genuinely married as we possibly can. But that doesn't mean *anything* is a given. How well or how poorly this goes is entirely dependent on how we approach it. You did sign a contract, and you did make a vow, and it *is* a little late for regrets—but if you have them . . ." He held his breath, then added, "Tell me now."

She looked at him as though she'd never seen him before. He was sure she was going to ask him to annul the marriage.

"I have no regrets," she said finally, her whole demeanor softening suddenly. She even pulled at the comb that held her elegant topknot in place. Gold silk fell around her shoulders in a rippling sheet. "I was just wondering," she admitted with a disarming little movement of her shoulder, "if I'll have them later. If . . . if we lose."

That hurt. "You mean because you made love with me for nothing?"

She blinked, apparently surprised and a little affronted by that suggestion. "Jeez, Jared! No. Because I am . . . attracted to you and because we've shared the care of the children I feel a certain . . . admiration for the way you deal with them and I know . . ." She was babbling, but she didn't seem able to stop. "I know sex isn't about the same things for a man, but I . . . I'll be investing real feelings in, you know, making love with you, and it's just a little unsettling to realize that it could all be over with a decision from the judge. I've . . . never been a woman who lived for the moment. I've always thought in the long term."

Jared appreciated her honesty, and couldn't remember a time when he'd been both so touched and so annoyed.

"Jeez yourself, Elizabeth!" he said a little too loudly. "And a few words of a stronger nature that I won't use in deference to our wedding night. I thought I made it clear the other night before your friends . . ." He stopped and waved a hand as though to wipe away that thought.

"Okay, let's not go there right now. I thought it would have been obvious to you that I have feelings for you, too. I don't understand them completely, primarily because there's been so little chance to indulge them with the kids around all the time and the employer-employee thing in our way. But I have...affection and respect for you, too, and I'm willing to invest them, as well."

They sat Indian-style, facing each other, and she watched the firelight highlight his dark hair, flicker in his eyes, burnish the line of his jaw. "I've always approached what I wanted to do with the belief that failure wasn't an option." He grinned ruefully. "Still, I've lost a few. But those are the stakes in life. You can sit in a rocking chair, or you can live."

So, he was reminding her that they could lose. But they could also win big time.

She couldn't help but wonder what would happen if he lost the children and she had to leave. Would life go on as it had when she'd been twenty-five, or would she be sent forward again, a failure past and future?

Well, she decided, perhaps it was time to live for the present if she didn't know where she would be spending her future.

She smiled, then looped her arms around Jared's neck. "That's very sane. But I'm giving you fair warning that I'm determined to mother those children, and I can be pretty convincing when I put my mind to it. So if you're really able to put that look in my eye and the judge believes us—then we're probably facing a lifetime of each other."

He rose to one knee, scooped her up in his arms and carried her to the bed. "Then it really is time," he said, setting her on her feet near the side of it, "that we get better acquainted."

He opened his mouth over hers and kissed her with that confident competence that had shaken the heart of her the last time. There was nothing so erotic in a man, she thought absently, her blood already beginning to simmer, as the assumption of control when he knew how to use it.

He slipped a hand under her sweater and splayed it against her back, pulling her to him. He kissed her again, his tongue delving, exploring, as his hand stroked her from the waistband of her pants to her shoulder. His touch was warm and strong and textured by the calluses he'd earned from hours spent in the workshop.

His hand roved her again, then brought the sweater up and off her. He unfastened the scrap of white lace that covered her breasts and tossed it at the chair with the discarded sweater.

Then he yanked his own shirt and T-shirt off and pulled her back to him.

She couldn't help the little groan of delight, of purely animal contentment when her soft breasts were re-shaped against the warm flesh that covered his rib cage. She said his name, stunned that this first flesh-to-flesh touch could feel so right.

Jared felt the pearled tips of her breasts against his chest and knew a sensation so strong he was sure they must have branded him. She was like an armful of silk and he couldn't stop stroking her. Her whispered cry of his name against his collarbone did nothing to slow him down.

He lifted her so that she stood on the edge of the bed. She grasped his shoulders for balance on the unsteady mattress as he unbuttoned and unzipped her pants and caught the waistband of her panties, drawing both down in a fluid sweep. She kicked them off.

Jared kissed the slight roundness of her and cupped her bottom in both hands. The flower-woman scent of her surrounded him, enfolded him, almost disoriented him. He felt her ragged sigh.

She drew his face to her stomach and held him there, letting her head fall back in the delicious perfection of the moment. She was rapidly forgetting all other reasons for being here except finally to know what would result from the fusion of their bodies. She'd wondered almost from the moment she'd met him.

She slipped to her knees and trapped his mouth with hers while she worked at the button and the zipper of his jeans. Her touch weakened him to putty.

It occurred to him, in a corner of his mind not completely occupied with sensual overload, that it was ironic that he'd been the one who'd talked about changing the look in *her* eyes. Because he no longer seemed familiar to himself. Who was this occupying his body so that a woman's touch paralyzed him? During a long and adventurous bachelorhood, he'd certainly been touched by women more accomplished than she.

But never by one more seemingly fascinated by him, more artful in her eager interest. That was an aphrodisiac beyond anything he'd ever known. When she slipped her hands between his hips and the jeans to push them down, the pleasure was exquisite.

He yanked them the rest of the way off and pulled her with him to the middle of the bed. He drew the blankets and the fuzzy quilt over them as the fire crackled and rain beat against the roof and the windows.

He drew her to him and her arms came around him, and he felt her lips at his collarbone, her knee slide up his thigh. He felt very literally like a time bomb.

Libby felt the reverence concentrated in his hands as they traced every curve of her, explored every hollow. His hands were everywhere, their movement over her exaggerating rather then satisfying a need that crept along her flesh, calling to him and moving on. Deep inside her a pulse began to tick.

Jared felt the tightening tension in her, the growing heat in her kisses and her touch. What he felt was so deep, so explosive, that he wondered in all fairness if he shouldn't give her one more chance to back out.

But he didn't know what he'd do if she took it. He suddenly felt as though all he'd ever been and done would cease to be when he finally entered her. That the mysteries of tomorrow were inside her, waiting for him.

So he rose over her, saw her eyes like flowers in the firelight as she positioned to receive him, and buried himself inside her with tender ruthlessness.

Libby adjusted to his possessive thrust, emitted a little cry of wonder at the perfection of it, and wrapped her body around him. He began to move inside her and she circled his hips in counterpoint, thinking this was almost too exquisite even to be.

Pleasure swelled out of the darkness, taunted her, ebbed away, only to rush toward her again, then retreat as she raised her hips to meet it.

Then Jared moved even deeper inside her and pleasure exploded, tossing her, turning her, pulling her down into a bottomless velvet well.

She was not at all surprised at the love that rose with her as she finally began to surface. She'd suspected it was there all along. But it had grown because of the way he treated the children, the way he loved his family.

Now she knew what it would be like to be the object of his love—and knew it was not a position she would ever abandon without a fight.

Jared, delighted in every little shudder that racked her body, was so focused on the way she whispered his name over and over that he experienced the broadside crash of his own pleasure almost with surprise.

She tightened her grip on him and he abandoned himself to joy, thinking as he spiraled farther and farther beyond that it was unsettling to be that out of control. Then her body tightened around his and he ceased to be able to think, feeling as though she'd drawn him into some soft, fragrant world from which he was powerless to escape. And neither did he want to.

"OHMIGOD!"

Jared, poking at the fire to satisfy himself that it was dying at shortly after two in the morning, heard Libby's shocked exclamation from the bathroom. They'd pillaged Darren's basket, made love a second time, finished the champagne, and were now getting serious about getting some sleep.

He pushed the door open without knocking, convinced by the tone of her voice that he'd find at least a rabid grizzly in there with her.

But she was alone, except for her reflection in the mirror. And that seemed to be what was troubling her. She leaned toward it over the sink, naked and graceful and completely distracting, her hair tumbled. He felt a curious catch in his chest. It occurred to him to worry about how vulnerable loving her made him.

He watched his own naked reflection as he wrapped his arms around her and drew her back against him. He kissed her temple and met her stunned blue eyes in the mirror.

"What?" he asked. "A wrinkle? A gray hair?"

"No." She sighed and leaned into him, a rueful acceptance in her expression as she continued to study herself. "Don't you see it?"

Because she seemed so serious, he concentrated on her reflection—and then he saw it. It was there in the slightly rounder curve of her cheeks caused by the little smile that wouldn't quite go away. And it was in her eyes. They were a little darker, as though reflecting deeper knowledge, deeper feeling, clearer understanding.

He'd done it. She looked like a well-loved woman. She looked like a wife.

He raised an eyebrow in self-satisfaction. "You're surprised?" he asked.

Her answer was to study his reflection.

Alert to what she was doing, he checked his own features and realized in alarm that he, too, looked changed. The arrogance was in place, along with the confidence he'd acquired early and accepted. But something had softened the lines of his jaw and his shoulder. Something had made him look...younger? Wiser? That wasn't even logical, but there'd been nothing cerebral about the night. Had he heard somewhere that the *heart* knew best?

She was watching his reflection in wonder, beginning to smile. "I did it to you, too," she whispered. "I made you look...loved."

He admitted to himself that he felt loved. In a night filled with startling revelations, that one took the prize.

Chapter Eleven

Shouts and screams came from Jared's house as he pulled into the driveway. Sure he was hearing things, he turned off the motor and raised a hand to shush Libby when she would have spoken to him.

And there it was, just audible in the ensuing silence—a high-pitched feminine voice and deeper masculine shouts carried on the brisk November air. The rain had washed away the pewter clouds, and the mid-afternoon sun was bright and golden.

"Was that...Darren's voice?" Libby asked, pushing her door open.

A feminine shout was clearly heard this time. "Well, where is she? Where *is* she?"

Libby turned to him sharply. "That was your mother."

Where was who? Considering his mother was watching his children, Jared headed for the house at a run, drawing the most obvious conclusion.

He found Carlie, Julio and Darren standing in an animated knot in the middle of the living room, all shouting at once in what could only be described as hysteria.

Near the fireplace, Justy paced with Zachary, who screamed at the top of his lungs.

"I *told* you it would help if you took her to the park this afternoon!" his mother was railing at his brother. "She had to be in all afternoon yesterday because of the rain. But nooo! You couldn't stop arguing with Justy long enough to help!"

"I *said* I'd take her!" Darren roared back. "But I was in the middle of . . ."

"The baby without marriage discussion. I know!"

"Mom!"

"Carlotta." Julio's rolling accent gave the name an exotic sound. "You must stop screaming. Darren did nothing to—"

Carlie rounded on him. "Don't you *dare* take his side! All I asked for was a little cooperation . . ."

"Yes, *cara,* but to you cooperation must always be on your terms. He—"

"What? Well, maybe you'd . . ."

"Mom!" Darren shouted, taking hold of her shoulders. "Forget my personal life! Forget taking sides! We've got to find Savannah!"

In the moment of stark silence that followed, Jared asked in a choked tone, "*Find* Savannah?" And as his family turned to him, surprised and horrified by his presence, he asked, his heart lurching uncomfortably, "You mean you've lost her?"

His mother began to sob. He heard Libby's intake of breath as she came up beside him.

Julio put an arm around her and said calmly, "I don't believe she is lost. Darren brought lunch, and we all ate together. That was only thirty minutes ago. I think she's playing. Hiding."

"But where?" Carlie demanded. "I've looked everywhere!"

Julio sighed patiently. "If I heard you screaming as you have been, I would not come out, either."

"I went to the workshop after lunch to see if that oak cabinet would fit in the restaurant's kitchen," Darren explained. "I think I'd have seen Savannah leave."

Libby, heart thumping, followed Jared as he ran through the kitchen and out the back, where only about ten yards of grassy sand separated them from the ocean. She'd walked with Savannah here on quiet afternoons. She looked up and down the beach, hoping the child had simply decided to walk on her own.

There was no sign of her. Reluctantly, she followed his gaze toward the water. The ocean was embroidered with sunlight, the waves gentle. There was no telltale evidence of her presence, no swatch of color on the waves, no waving arm. But would there have been if she'd walked into the water, unaware that . . .

Then she heard Jared's swift, pithy curse. She turned, as did Carlie, Julio, Darren and Justy, who'd trailed them outside.

Jared was looking up. She followed his gaze and saw Savannah standing on the railing of the little porchlike detail outside her bedroom window two stories up. She held the window frame for support.

Carlie opened her mouth to shriek, but Julio covered the sound with his hand. Libby felt her own instinctive cry strangle in her throat as Jared and Darren ran into the house.

Savannah saw her and smiled cheerfully. She freed one hand to wave, then lost her balance and flailed the air.

"Savannah!" Libby said her name on a gasp. "Hold on with both hands!" She pushed against the air, as though she could reach her and hold her there.

Julio ran to stand under the little porch. "Hold on, *cara!*" he called.

The upstairs window opened and Jared crawled out into the narrow space.

"Daddy!" Savannah was still smiling. "I was flying to find Mommy. Like Rosie!"

He had to walk sideways, crablike, to reach her. In an instant he had her and handed her to Darren, who hung halfway out the window.

Carlie threw her arms around Libby and wept. Julio came to put his arms around both of them. "See, now. All is well that ends without difficulty."

Carlie sniffed and held on.

And that was when Libby noticed the round-faced, redheaded woman standing just beyond them, clutching a file folder and a yellow pad. She wore glasses, a khaki-colored raincoat and an apologetic smile.

"Hello," she said. "I'm Genevieve Griffin from Children's Services. I found the front door open and followed the voices." Her glance went to Savannah's second-story perch. "I'm a day early, but I had a schedule change and hoped you wouldn't mind." She looked upward to where Savannah had been. "You seem to be having quite a day."

Libby gazed heavenward with a "Take me now Lord" plea and waited for lightning to strike, or for some fortuitous tsunami to pull her out to sea. But her prayer went unanswered.

Forced with having to cope, she dredged up a smile from somewhere and led the way inside. She could hear

Carlie and Julio arguing quietly behind them as Genevieve Griffin talked about how much she loved the coast and what a treat it was to visit.

In the house, Justy handed Libby the screaming baby and excused herself. "Darren and I'll make coffee."

"But I wanted to expl—" Darren began, but Justy pulled him with her toward the kitchen. "Carlie, you want to help?"

"No, I want to tell Miss Griffin . . ."

But Julio caught her hand and pulled her to follow Justy and Darren.

Jared, with Savannah riding his arm and looking somewhat chastened, intercepted them in the middle of the living room. He extended his free hand. "Mrs. Griffin," he said. Libby exchanged a look of wry despair with him. "I didn't see you come in."

She explained how she'd walked into an empty house. "I believe you were doing a high-wire act when I arrived," she said with a smile. She had to speak loudly to be heard over Zachary's screams.

Libby went to kiss Savannah's cheek. "Sweetie, are you all right?"

Savannah looked put out. "Daddy yelled at me," she complained.

"Well, you mustn't climb out the window like that. You could have fallen and gotten hurt."

Savannah folded little arms argumentatively. "I was gonna fly."

"Fly," Genevieve Griffin repeated worriedly.

"Like Rosie in Libby's book," Jared said. "It's a long story. Would you like to sit down?"

"Excuse me a minute, please." Libby backed away toward the kitchen. "I'll get Zachary a bottle. That ought to quiet him down."

The kitchen was a hive of silent activity. No one seemed to be speaking to anyone. Justy was pouring water in the coffee maker's well, Darren stood over a whirring microwave, Carlie was putting cream and sugar on a tray and Julio sloshed hot water in the shamrock-sprigged coffee server.

Everyone turned to her when she walked into the room. Carlie hurried to take the baby from her while she ran a bottle under hot water.

"We have to explain that it was all our fault!" Darren insisted. "After what that woman saw this afternoon, she'll yank the kids from you for sure."

"Darren!" Justy admonished.

"Well, it's true," Carlie sniffed, large tears sliding down her cheeks as she held Zachary to her and rocked him. "It was all *my* fault. I left her coloring because I wanted to wash out bedding and . . ."

"Please, Carlie." Libby looked at her over her shoulder as she wiped off the bottle. "I've been around Savannah long enough to know she can be gone in a minute. I'm sure Jared will be able to explain."

And apparently he had. When Libby returned to the living room with a much happier baby greedily sucking on his bottle, she found Jared and Mrs. Griffin in what appeared to be a very amiable conversation.

"A couple of weeks doesn't seem like a very long acquaintance," he was saying, "but we had the children in common and that seemed to accelerate our attraction to each other. We were married yesterday."

"Well. My goodness." Mrs. Griffin appeared surprised, but not unpleasantly so. "We do like to be kept informed of these things, but I guess we can intrude only so far." She turned to smile at the gulping baby in Libby's arms. "He certainly seems much happier."

"He missed lunch," Libby explained, "while Savannah was missing."

Savannah, apparently over her pique, pointed to Jared and told Mrs. Griffin, "This is my daddy."

The caseworker smiled. "Yes, I know."

"My other one died in the car."

"Yes."

"I was going to fly to find my mommy."

"You mean . . . fly to heaven?" Mrs. Griffin asked.

"Not that mommy," Savannah corrected. Then she pointed to Libby. "Her!"

Libby blinked.

"They had a wedding," Savannah explained for the caseworker's benefit. "Now I have a daddy *and* a mommy. Just like before. Want to see my room?"

"Sure." Mrs. Griffin stood and offered her hand, and Savannah hauled her upstairs.

Jared took Zachary from Libby and they followed. "Well, didn't you make a good impression?" he teased softly as they went up the stairs. "Quiet the screaming baby and go from nanny to mommy just like that."

Libby beamed. "I'm good at this."

Jared arched an eyebrow. "You're good at a lot of things."

Savannah explained in laborious and animated detail about Rosie and Tux and how they flew at night to find out where her mother's latest trip had taken her.

"And in the nighttime," Savannah said, "the stars twinkle 'cause Libby did it with special paint."

"Well." Mrs. Griffin glanced around her at the room that had everything in it a child could want and spread her arms. "This does look like as perfect a situation as one could hope for for two little children."

"You're not upset about the . . . ?" Libby pointed to the window.

Mrs. Griffin laughed lightly. "My son once drove our car to the movies."

When Jared and Libby did not react with appropriate shock, she added with a roll of her eyes, "He was ten at the time. I know children are quick and the effort to keep them safe can often defy the efforts of the most vigilant of us. What we watch for in placing children is the development of a comfort and satisfaction in the everydayness of their lives. And I certainly see that here. Savannah seems very comfortable with both of you. Enough so that she's willing to move on with her life. What more can we ask?"

"Have you met Lady Barmont?" Jared asked.

She sighed. "Yes. She seems like a nice woman who'd like to make up for what she's done to her family in the past by raising her sister's children. Her parents have been gone for some time." She eyed Libby's border. "If she had her way, Paris, Rome and London would be part of Savannah's everyday reality."

Jared and Libby exchanged a grim glance.

She smiled from one to the other. "But I'm going to give you high enough marks to try to tip the scales in your favor despite her blood connection. Have faith."

Carlie insisted on walking Mrs. Griffin to her car and assuming the blame for Savannah's mishap.

"I'm so sorry," she told Jared after the woman had left. She wrapped her arms around him and hugged him tightly. "I don't know what I'll do if that hurts your case."

He patted her back consolingly. "She seemed to understand. And she was pleased generally with Savannah's adjustment."

Carlie breathed a sigh of relief. "I certainly hope so. How was the bed-and-breakfast?"

Jared saw the interest in his mother's eyes. She wanted to believe that his decision to marry Libby had been based on more than the need to present to the court a mother for his children.

And he was sure it had been, now that he thought about it. But he had a long history of taunting her by withholding information.

"Very comfortable," he said. He turned to Libby, who seemed also to have read his mother's mind and was doing her best to maintain a straight face. "Wasn't it?"

"Very," she confirmed. "The woman who runs it makes her own bagels. Imagine that."

Carlie shook her head at Libby in exasperation. "Married to him one day, and already he's gotten to you. I don't want details, I just want to know that you...were able to relax, talk about...what people who are going to spend a lifetime together talk about."

Darren pulled his mother away from Jared and took her place. "Forget talk. *I* want details."

Julio appeared beside Carlie. He had Zachary on his shoulder. "Did I hear there are going to be details? Speak slowly, please. My English is still a little rough."

Jared laughed, Carlie put a horrified hand to her mouth, Justy covered her eyes and Darren hooked an arm around Julio's shoulders. "You know, you're okay, Julio. You're going to be all right as a stepfather."

Jared had to agree. Knowing his mother would be loved by this kind and caring man with an active sense of humor would make up in part for her being far away.

Darren turned to Justy. "Don't you want details?"

She smiled blandly at her employer. "Absolutely. Let's have them. Did you bathe in champagne? Do it on the dresser? What?"

Jared was accustomed to his family's and Justy's incessant teasing, but he'd learned something about himself last night that made taking it lightly difficult.

He turned to Libby, wondering if she was embarrassed, if she needed him to put a stop to this. But he saw that her eyes were alight with laughter. She slipped her arm around his waist and leaned into his shoulder with an ease that pleased him.

"Let's just say," she said with a certain primness he knew to be out of character and strictly for their audience's benefit, "that we made excellent use of the pâté."

Darren and Julio hooted and exchanged a high five. Justy giggled and Carlie opened her arms to encompass Jared and Libby. "I'm thrilled to know there's hope for you!" she exclaimed.

Jared exchanged an ironic look with Libby, both of them amused that everyone *thought* they were kidding.

Carlie stood back to announce, "You understand, of course, that you have Julio and I as houseguests until the court date. I can't go home until I know the children are yours."

He had no problem with that. He wanted to believe that things would go well and they would need help celebrating.

"Great," he said. "You can help me sort through a box of metalwork fixtures, see if there's anything you'll want for your shop. Julio? Can you deal with this for a couple of days?"

"Of course," he replied with a courtly bow. "I am in for the long . . . what is it?"

"Long haul?" Darren suggested.

Julio frowned. "Hall? As a dance hall?"

"No," Darren corrected. "Haul. *H-a-u-l,* as to pull."

Julio thought about that a moment, then smiled. "To pull things together?"

"Yes!" Darren applauded his perception.

"Like us," Justy added, putting an arm around Carlie and one around Darren. "Pulling together so that Jared and Libby get the children."

"I understand." Julio put an arm around Darren and one around Jared, who still held Libby to him. "We are backs united."

Darren tried to interpret that and apparently failed; he turned to Jared. Jared winced and considered the words, trying to make sense of them.

"A united *front?*" Justy asked.

"Yes! That is it!"

"I hope this thing works out between Justy and me," Darren whispered to Jared. "When Julio marries Mom, we're going to need her as an interpreter."

LIBBY STOOD in the middle of the children's room at just after two the morning of their court date. She'd spent the past ten minutes going from Savannah's bed to

Zachary's crib, absorbing the reality of their presence in her life.

She couldn't fathom what her future could hold without them, without their father. How could it go on in such paltry circumstances when she'd known such riches with them? It didn't seem possible.

Warm hands came down on her shoulders out of the darkness, but instead of frightening her, they provided her with the comfort she couldn't find within herself. She knew Jared's touch so well now after just a week of marriage. She knew every artful and tender fingertip, the protective quality in his palm, the strength in the grip that now wrapped her against him.

"You're not giving up, are you?" he murmured against her ear.

"No," she replied softly, but a large tear fell onto his hand, belying her denial. She wanted to believe, but she'd been orphaned as a teenager, tossed around by time and claimed by a pair of children. She knew things could happen over which one had no control.

She wrapped one arm around his, then pointed to the dark, moonless sky beyond the window. The clear, sunny days had finally given way to the more usual cold and rain. "There isn't even a star to wish on tonight."

He kissed the side of her neck. "Yes, there is. I have you right here in my arms. You've brought light to my days and my nights and every... every itchy, unsatisfied corner of my being. You wouldn't have been dropped into my life if I hadn't been meant to keep the children."

She wanted to believe that. She turned in his arms to look up at him. His eyes and his smile shone in the shadowy room. "You had them before I came into it," she reminded him.

He nodded. "But you saw how I was doing. You taught me how to enjoy them, how to give to them. How to take what they offer." He kissed her soundly and crushed her to him. "But you've become a part of me in a way that has nothing to do with them. You belong to me as my lover, as my wife, not just as their mother. Do you understand?"

She clung to him, her heartbeat accelerating. Did he mean what she thought she was hearing?

He sensed her uncertainty and clarified it for her. He wouldn't voice the thought that the children might be taken from them, so he said, instead, "I'm not ever letting you go, Libby. Nothing's going to take you from me. Nothing. Ever."

She began to sob, happiness and pain a tangle in her chest.

He lifted her into his arms and carried her back to his room. He placed her in the middle of the bed, climbed in beside her and held her tightly.

She cried her heart out and he let her, because he knew the only true control he had over this situation was his own conviction that Savannah and Zachary were his and nothing would separate him from them.

If he followed the logic of that, he had once thought Mandy was his, and he'd lost her. But now, having known Libby, he understood that it hadn't been love at all that he'd lost. It had been something more selfish, less substantial. He hadn't known what love was then.

What he felt for Libby and the children had changed the look in his eyes. Surely a judge would see that.

THE COURTHOUSE in Portland was a genteel remnant of a historic past. The mahogany-panelled lobby opened onto various offices, then swept toward a wide marble stairway that led to courtrooms and judges' chambers. Libby and Jared climbed them holding Savannah between them. She lifted her feet at every other step, swinging between them gleefully. Savannah thought of the day as an exciting family outing.

Since Mrs. Griffin had assured them that even if the judge's decision did go against them, it would be several days before Savannah and Zachary would be moved, they'd decided against telling her the reason for the visit to the judge.

Carlie, Julio, Darren and Justy followed, Darren carrying Zachary.

A slender, middle-aged woman greeted them in the judge's office, then guided Jared and Libby and the children into the judge's chambers.

"I'm afraid the rest of the family will have to wait here," she told Carlie when she would have followed.

Julio pulled her back toward a bank of chairs. "Come, *cara,*" he said. "We will sit here with Darren and Justine and be the united front."

The judge was a tall, bulky man with a receding hairline and shrewd brown eyes. He greeted them with a courteous but professional distance Libby guessed had to go with the job.

He asked questions about their employment and their new marriage. He raised an eyebrow when he calculated that the ceremony had taken place after Lady Barmont had appeared on the horizon.

"Jared hired me as the children's nanny," Libby explained, careful not to look at Jared. Technically, that *was* the truth. She hadn't said she *was* a nanny. "And we fell in love."

The judge flipped a page on his report. "After two weeks?" He looked up at Jared.

Jared met his gaze. "I was in love with her in two days," he said. "I waited two weeks to give her time to adjust to the idea."

The judge studied him with damnably unrevealing eyes. Then he turned to Libby.

"And how long did it take you?"

She smiled because this answer was really true. "Until the first time I saw him deal with Zachary during a sleepless night. It takes a big man—a big anybody—to remember the baby's needs and not your own when you've been up twenty hours."

The judge smiled fractionally. "We had colicky twins. I know what you mean." He grew serious again. "So you're telling me two single people accustomed to doing what they want when they want and with a freedom this decision could change inextricably and forever are willing to turn their lives upside down for two little children?"

Libby shrugged. "Actually, Jared and the children have turned my life right side up. So yes, I am."

The judge allowed himself another small smile and faced Jared. "And you?"

"Yes."

"Right side up or upside down?"

Jared laughed softly. "Depends on which day you catch me. But every day they make it all worthwhile."

The judge made a few notes on his report, then turned his attention to Savannah. "What did you have for breakfast, Savannah?'' he asked with a cheerful grin.

"Eggs Ben-a-dick," she replied, banging together the toes of the patent-leather shoes sticking straight out ahead of her.

The judge blinked and turned to Libby. "Eggs Benedict? Really?"

Libby pointed to Jared. "Jared's brother is a chef. Savannah loves his cooking. He came over this morning to provide . . . moral support."

"He's waiting out there with Grandma." Savannah pointed to the door through which they'd come.

"Do you like your new house?" he asked.

Savannah nodded. "I have Rosie and Tux on the wall and stars that twinkle up high. Libby made them."

Jared explained about Libby's artistic abilities and the border project.

The judge raised an eyebrow. "And what if you sell your book," he asked Libby, "then find that the care of two small children puts some of your goals out of your reach?"

"Then I'll be like every other working mother in the world." She smiled as Savannah came to scramble up into her lap. "Actually, I imagine it'll be easier to write books for children with children surrounding me."

The judge refocused his attention on Savannah. "Do you like living with Jared and Libby, Savannah?" he asked.

"Yeah," she replied gravely. "My other mom and dad went to heaven. But I can't go there yet. So I'm gonna stay with them." Her mood changed with a sudden bright smile. "And this time I have a grandma and a uncle."

The judge's expression grew warmly indulgent. "What do you like to do best?"

Savannah launched into a litany that seemed without end. "Painting, walking with Libby on the beach, wearing Daddy's goggles in the workshop, playing with Spike and Tippy and Scarlett, cooking with Uncle..."

The judge leaned back, a smile on his face as she carried on at length. When she finally finished with the regret that she couldn't curl his hair because her things were at home, the judge closed his folder, then stood and held a pen across the desk to Jared and turned a legal document toward him. "Sign there. The first *X*."

"What is it?" Jared asked, scanning the small, tight print. "Affixed hereto this twentieth day of November..." he began reading.

"The adoption papers," the judge replied.

Jared's head came up in surprise. He heard Libby's little gasp. The judge came around the desk to take the baby from her. "You, too, Mrs. Ransom. Sign the second *X*."

"What about Mrs. Barmont?" Jared asked.

Zachary made conversational noises and the judge bounced him around on his hip, the professional neutrality suddenly gone. "Withdrew her petition this morning. Seems her therapist advised her against it, that she wasn't doing it for the right reasons or something. Anyway, she changed her mind. But I wanted to learn a little about you before going with Mrs. Griffin's overzealous report. She seems to think you should both be canonized." He touched his first two fingertips to his forehead. "But I think just a friendly salute from one parent to another will do it. Good luck."

There were tears and cheers in the judge's outer office when the family heard the news.

Savannah and Zachary were hugged and passed around and kissed and promised treats.

Darren insisted on taking everyone to dinner. "This is your town, Libby," he said. "Where'll we go?"

"Truffles!" Libby replied without hesitation. "Sara and Charlene and I used to go there all the time." She turned to Jared. "Do you mind if I call and ask them to join us?" She grabbed the lapels of his jacket and pulled him close. "They'll be so excited about how everything is working out."

He kissed her, his heart swollen with happiness and goodwill. "Of course not. I'm excited myself. We'll all stay at the Rockland tonight and drive home in the morning." He looked at their companions. "Okay with everyone?"

The endorsement was unanimous.

Chapter Twelve

Over dinner they planned Carlie and Julio's wedding to take place the following week at Jared's since they'd all be together for Thanksgiving anyway, and accepted with equanimity the news that Darren and Justy were moving in together.

Carlie offered her good wishes, then focused on Justy. "You know you were my choice for a daughter-in-law years ago, and I'm afraid my feelings haven't changed. You'll forgive me if I root for marriage to result from this."

"Of course," Justy, holding Zachary, said amiably. "Just try to remember that I'm not the marrying kind."

Carlie pointed to Jared and Libby. "But you're getting together to have a baby. Haven't you noticed what can happen when two people share children?"

"This is different."

"How?"

Darren grinned at his mother and reached across the table to pat her hand. "Because Justy's involved. Let it go, Mom."

Carlie sighed. "Do I still get to claim the baby as my grandchild?"

"Of course." Justy elbowed Darren affectionately. "We'll all be family."

That declaration did not fit the parameters she'd set, but Jared was happy when his mother let the matter drop. He knew Darren to be stubborn and determined and lionhearted when it came to working for what he believed in. Darren had a plan at work here, and Jared trusted him to see it through. He could only pray for a favorable outcome.

Jared sat back as Libby chatted animatedly with Sara and Charlene. Savannah came around the table and climbed into his lap, rubbing her eyes. She curled up against him with an ease and confidence he'd once wondered if he'd be able to inspire.

She and Zachary were his. Theirs. He'd been unable to imagine any other outcome; still, he couldn't quite believe how easily it had been accomplished.

Three weeks ago he'd been a bachelor fishing in Scotland. Today he had a wife and two children. He smiled to himself as he speculated on what tomorrow might bring.

Libby turned to him, her eyes vibrant and happy. Her hair was loose and tucked behind her ear on one side, revealing her slender neck and lending her an air of fragility he knew to be completely false. He felt joy so deep it hurt.

"Want me to take her," she asked, "so you can finish your coffee?"

He ran a knuckle down her cheek because he just had to touch her. "I'm fine."

Her eyes trailed over his face with a smoldering quality that made him long for the time when they would be alone tonight.

"You're getting awfully good at being a father."

He accepted her praise with a modest inclination of his head. "I told you I'd get the hang of it."

She leaned closer as everyone else around the table paired off in their conversations. "You're also a great husband," she said softly, her lips inches from his. Her eyes grew serious. "I can't believe you belong to me."

He closed the gap that separated them and kissed her lightly. "I thought *you* belonged to *me.*"

She leaned her cheek against his and murmured in his ear, "I do. Wholeheartedly." She drew back slightly to look into his eyes, her own soft with love. "I do, Jared. I love you."

He kissed her again, Savannah asleep and clutched between them. "You own my soul," he said softly against her lips. "I love you, too."

Libby heard the words with wonder. She'd been right! She hadn't failed after all. She'd been sent back to reclaim her children and had been blessed with the exquisite bonus of a loving man. She felt humbled by God's generosity.

Darren cleared his throat noisily. "Shall we order pâté to go?" he asked, indicating their obvious intimacy.

Jared and Libby drew apart slowly, shared a long, promising look. Then Jared gave Darren a grinning glance as he reached for his wallet. "We'll just trust that there's some in the honor bar in the room. Everybody ready?"

They moved in a body toward the door, Libby admiring a rich red-and-gold paisley scarf Charlene threw carelessly over the shoulder of her coat.

"I love scarves," Libby said as they made their way to the door. "But I never know what to do with them."

Charlene hugged her happily. "As long as you know what to do with the pâté," she whispered. "Be happy!"

Libby could not imagine being happier than she was at that moment with Jared beside her, carrying the now-sleeping Savannah. Justy and Darren followed, with Darren holding Zachary in the carrier and Carlie and Julio joining them with youthful joy in their eyes. And this was all hers!

She hugged Sara, then walked her down to where Charlene waited for her car. At the top of the steps, Carlie helped Jared work Savannah's coat onto the child's inert body.

Libby, Sara and Charlene shared a three-way hug, then her two friends climbed into the car. Libby didn't notice Charlene's scarf until the taillights of her car illuminated it. She leaned down to pick it up, turning to shout at the departing car, hoping to stop it.

At that same moment there was a strange ticking sound behind her, a desperate shout of "Laaaadyyyy!" and a single light coming at her with a speed that made escape impossible.

No, she thought, cold dread seeping into her limbs, immobilizing her. *Not again.*

The impact rattled her teeth and robbed her breath and she went down with the tortured sound of Jared's shout on the cold night air.

JARED SAW Libby dart away from the side of the driveway into the very middle just as the messenger's bike sped around an aisle of parked cars and headed for the exit—and Libby.

He shouted her name at the same moment that she turned at the sound of the bike's brakes. But she seemed transfixed there. His heart stopped when the bike hit her with a sickening thump. The rider went over the handlebars, and Libby lay lifelessly in the middle of the driveway, the bike on top of her, its wheels spinning. Julio snatched Savannah from him and he ran toward Libby, wondering how in God's name he'd go on if he lost her.

LIBBY FELT a subtle ache behind her eyes and knew that opening them would be painful. She remembered drinking wine the night before to celebrate the adoption, but she'd had only one glass. Why should she feel . . . ?

An image of a speeding light flashed suddenly in her mind's eye. She saw it coming toward her, heard Jared's shout. She groaned, remembering the maniac messenger who'd hit her the last time, and presumed she'd been felled by him again.

The last time! Libby opened her eyes and sat up abruptly, ignoring the throbbing in her head. Her heart thudded and her breath grew shallow as she recalled what had happened the last time she'd awakened in a hospital.

She sat still, trying to assess her situation. Despite the pain in her head, all her senses seemed heightened, razor sharp, as though she'd just awakened from a dream.

As the possible ramifications of that thought came home to her, panic bubbled up. A dream. No. Oh, no.

She looked around herself, searching desperately for landmarks in time and reality. She saw acoustical tiles, pale-green walls, white curtains. She stared at the spot where the red smiley face had been the last time.

It wasn't there. *Oh, no.*

Nausea rose beside the panic on a rolling wave.

She spotted the clock above the chair. It read 11:17, but was it the morning after last night, or was she back in her lonely future? Or had she never left it and merely dreamed her life with Jared and the children?

Time seemed to stop, to bend, to warp as she struggled to right her mind, to clear her thoughts, to *believe* that she hadn't lost her husband and her children—that she hadn't lost her life, her world.

No, she prayed. *Please, God. Please let me be back there. Please don't let this be where I was before you let me have Jared and the children. Please!*

The door opened and a pretty young nurse walked in. She came to take Libby's pulse. "How are we doing this morning?" she asked in a cheerful voice.

"Fine," Libby replied, her voice thick with panic. "Where's Farthingale?"

"Gone," the nurse replied, without moving her eyes from her watch.

"When?"

"Ages ago."

No!

The nurse looked up at her and frowned. "Whoa! Your pulse is galloping. Let me . . ."

"No!" Libby pushed her away, threw back the covers and ran for the door, feeling as though the life was being squeezed out of her body. As she passed the open bathroom door, she caught a glimpse of her reflection in the mirror and stopped in her tracks, all her bodily functions suspended.

Her hair was short, skimmed over her ears and fringed at her nape. Short! No!

Everything inside her screamed. She was the thirty-five-year-old Libby again. She had lost Jared and Savannah and Zachary. And not just lost them to someone else, but *lost* them in time.

Or she'd simply wanted them so much that she'd dreamed them to life, then loved them so much the dream had become her reality. Oh, God.

She felt as though her heart had been ripped out. She remembered sitting on the sofa with Jared's arm around her, Savannah climbing over them and the baby locked between them, and felt a loss so profound she couldn't stop a wail of despair.

She leaned against the molding and sank to the carpet, sure she would die. She was vaguely aware of the nurse running from the room.

She heard her cry turn to sobs as the sense of loss buffeted her like some title-holding, bare-fisted boxer.

Then there was a sudden commotion in the room, and a pair of strong arms scooped her off the carpet and carried her back to the bed.

The familiarity of the touch, the scent, the muscle penetrated her grief, and she stopped sobbing abruptly to stare with complete shock into Jared's face.

She was hallucinating. She had to be. Unless he'd come forward in time with her—or out of the dream.

She put her fingertips to deep worry lines on his forehead and felt warm flesh, the wiry hair of his eyebrows, the brush of his rough chin against the inside of her wrist.

He'd shed the suit coat and tie he'd had on at dinner, and his collar was open. He had an overnight beard and his eyes looked bleary and miserable—and so real and alive that confusion was suspended for an instant while she simply stared in wonder.

"Jared?" she finally whispered.

"Yes," he answered. He sat beside her and held her forearms. "Are you all right?"

She shook her head, trying to clear it. "What are you doing...here?"

He blinked, apparently surprised by the question. "I'm your husband, remember? I'm supposed to be where you are. Don't you remember getting hurt?" He looked at the doctor in concern. The doctor, who must have followed Jared into the room, sat on the other side of Libby, with the nurse hovering nearby.

The doctor pushed her gently back to the pillows, but she resisted, trying to hold on to Jared. "But it's ten years later, isn't it?" she asked.

Jared helped the doctor push her back but held her hand as the doctor took her pulse and listened to her heart. Then he asked gently, "Later than what, my love?"

"Later than yesterday!" she replied, her voice high and urgent.

He frowned at her worriedly. "Libby, it's Saturday. Remember yesterday at the courthouse? We signed the papers to adopt Zack and Savannah?"

"You mean...*they're* here?" she asked in disbelief.

"They're in the waiting room with Mom and Julio and everybody else."

"*They're* here, too?" She sat up, but Jared pushed her back again. "And...everybody else?"

"Yes. Darren, Justy, Sara, Charlene? Don't you remember that we all had dinner at Truffles?"

And that was when the doubts began to creep into her muddled brain. They couldn't all have come forward in time—or out of a dream.

The doctor withdrew his stethoscope, looped it around the back of his neck and shook his head. "Her pulse is fast, but generally I think she's all right. Except that's something's obviously upset her. What happened, Libby?"

She put her hand to her face, trying to remember, trying to sort through what she remembered of the night before.

Jared turned to sit behind her and wrap an arm around her. "You had a good bump, Libby. If you're confused, there's good reason for it. It's okay. Tell us what upset you."

She winced and leaned into him gratefully. He was here—wherever he'd come from. He was here. She hadn't lost him. That knowledge drew all her concentration for a moment, then she tried again to put the past in order. But where was it? And had it been real?

"She looked in the mirror," the nurse said, "and that seemed to upset her. And she asked for Farthingale."

Farthingale! Libby sat up and asked the doctor, "How many years has Farthingale been retired?"

He raised an eyebrow. "She isn't retired. Not for another month."

Libby uttered a gasp of surprise and reminded the nurse, "You said she'd been gone for ages."

"She has," the nurse replied, mildly defensive. "She worked three to eleven. She'd been gone almost twelve hours when you asked. To me that seemed—" she shrugged apologetically "—ages. I never thought you'd think I meant *years*."

"Okay." She pointed to the spot on the opposite wall where the smiling graffiti had been. "Where's the red smiley face that used to be there?"

"It still is," the nurse replied. "In room 231. This is 237."

Oh, dear. Libby leaned back against Jared with a thunk. "You're going to think this is a crazy question but . . . how old am I?"

"Twenty-five," he replied. "I saw it on your birth certificate when we got our marriage license."

"I was born in . . ."

"Nineteen seventy-one. Twenty-five years ago. On Saint Patrick's Day."

She frowned and rubbed her forehead. "But I . . . used to be . . . thirty-five." She looked up at Jared, pleading with him to understand. "I missed my appointment with John Miller because I was hit by a bicycle, and I went back ten years in time to find that you'd taken the kids and . . ."

The doctor smiled and tipped his head back as though he'd just had a revelation. "Is that it?" He leaned toward Libby and said earnestly, "I took care of you three weeks ago when you had that first bump, remember? You *dreamed* about being thirty-five. I remember because I was reading your chart while you were still out of it, and you were singing 'Happy Birthday' to yourself, then I heard you say, 'Thirty-five! God, that's ancient.' I recall that clearly because, being *fifty*-five, I was amused by it."

She closed her eyes and tried to absorb that. "You mean, I *dreamed* being older? That I never was thirty-five? But it was so real. When I woke up, I thought I'd gone backward in time to . . . to get the children."

Jared held her tightly. "Why would a dream confuse her like that?"

The doctor shrugged. "Dreams can seem very real. We can wake up from scary ones perspiring and with our hearts pounding. And she wanted something very desperately at the time—the children. There was talk about her in Pediatrics, how she'd bonded with the children and wanted to adopt them. That was probably all on her mind when she sustained the blow."

He sighed and spread his hands—an indicator, Libby guessed, that some things couldn't be completely explained.

"The brain is complex and mysterious. Even the specialists don't know how or why it sifts and organizes data. My guess is that the blow combined with the trauma of the children caused a glitch. And it could very well be that this second blow straightened it out. But it might be a good idea to set her up with a therapist to be sure."

Libby wanted to believe that this was her present, had always been her present, but there were a few problems remaining.

"How do you account for my hair?" she asked, arms folded. "It was short when I was thirty-five. It's short now."

She felt Jared's light laughter against her and turned her head to look up at him. He was smiling. He hadn't smiled since he'd walked into the room.

"When you went down with the bike," he explained, "the wheels were still spinning, and your hair got caught in the spokes. There wasn't time to untangle it, obviously, so I told the EMT to cut it and get you in the ambulance."

She stared at him for a moment, struggling to regain her emotional equilibrium.

"I actually did dream being thirty-five?" she asked, unable to believe it was all still hers. "And we're really married? And the judge...gave us the children?"

He held up her left hand, where a wide gold band circled her third finger. "See?" He held up his own left hand. "Matches mine. And the kids are right outside. Want me to bring them in?" He looked at the doctor for an okay.

"Sure." The doctor stood. "I'll make her an appointment for sometime next week with Dr. Gilder to talk over what happened and track the next few weeks, but she can go home. She's fine."

The doctor and the nurse left, but Libby caught Jared's arm before he could go to the door to get the children.

"Wait," she said. "There's one more thing."

He came back to her and took her hand, his eyes gentle. "What is it?"

"Well...when I was...when I *thought* I was thirty-five...there was a man. We weren't intimate or anything, but I thought of him as...real."

"Real enough to have a name?"

"Yes. Boris Pushkin." Even as she said the name, she knew she'd had *some* connection with him in the past.

Jared smiled again, even laughed. "The brain is mysterious." He pinched her chin. "He's your editor."

She winced, trying to remember. "I don't have an editor." But...was that the name to whom she'd addressed her manuscript?

"You do now," he corrected. "I called home this morning to get my messages, and he had called. Wants you to call him to talk about your book."

She felt her eyes grow wide. "To...*buy* it?"

"He didn't say that, but I imagine that's the kind of news they don't like to leave on an answering machine."

"Ohmigod!"

He wrapped his arms around her and rubbed gently between her shoulder blades. "Now, don't get your pulse up again, or the doctor won't let me take you home. And if I have to live another night without you, I'll go berserk."

"Oh, Jared." She sighed against him, leaning into his embrace, feeling everything clarify and stabilize for her in his arms. "I love you so much. I thought I was going to die when I woke up and thought I'd left you and the children behind."

He kissed her neck and held her tighter. "You couldn't lose me, Libby. Even in time. I'd go backward, forward, sideways, even to Hell for you. But I intend to hold you so tightly you won't get away from me—ever."

She could think of no sweeter, more reassuring promise than that.

"Want to see the children now?"

"Please."

Jared stood back while Savannah scrambled onto the bed and into Libby's arms, chattering nonstop about the nurses she remembered from three weeks ago and the teddy bears they'd given her and Zachary that morning.

Libby's face lit up, her earlier confusion apparently vanquished by the child's obvious delight in being with her again.

Darren put Zachary in Libby's arms, and he and Justy, his mother and Julio and Sara and Charlene crowded around her, pouring love over her in invisible, healing buckets.

His happiness was so complete he almost couldn't believe his good fortune. But it was such a boisterous happiness it had to be real.

He wondered for a moment about what Libby had experienced, then dismissed it as she reached a hand out for him to draw him toward her. Past. Future. Dream. Reality. It didn't matter what this was. It had his wife and children in it—and the rest of his family. He claimed it as his.

HARLEQUIN®

AMERICAN ◆ ROMANCE®
®

gift-wrapped
GROOMS

What better present
this Christmas than
four handsome, sexy
Gift-Wrapped Grooms
under the tree—just for you!

Imagine spending those long,
cold winter evenings snuggled up
with guys like Lucky, Cole, Sam
and Nick.... Next month don't miss:

#657 THE LITTLEST ANGEL:
Charlotte Maclay

#658 COLE IN MY STOCKING:
Jule McBride

#659 ANOTHER NEW YEAR'S EVE:
Phyllis Houseman

#660 THREE WISE MEN & A BABY:
Jenna McKnight

Coming in December, only from
Harlequin American Romance

Look us up on-line at: http://www.romance.net

GWG

HARLEQUIN ®

Scandals

A passionate story of romance, where bold, daring characters
set out to defy their world of propriety and strict social codes.

"Scandals—a story that will make your heart race and your
pulse pound. Spectacular!"   —Suzanne Forster

"Devon is daring, dangerous and altogether delicious."
                                       —Amanda Quick

Don't miss this wonderful full-length novel from Regency
favorite Georgina Devon.

Available in December, wherever Harlequin books are sold.

Look us up on-line at: http://www.romance.net

Merry Christmas, Baby!

A romantic collection filled with the magic
of Christmas and the joy of children.

SUSAN WIGGS, Karen Young and
Bobby Hutchinson bring you Christmas wishes,
weddings and romance, in a charming
trio of stories that will warm up your
holiday season.

MERRY CHRISTMAS, BABY! also contains
Harlequin's special gift to you—a set of
FREE GIFT TAGS included in every book.

Brighten up your holiday season with
MERRY CHRISTMAS, BABY!

Available in November at
your favorite retail store.

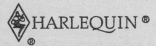

MCB

1997
Reader's Engagement Book
A calendar of important dates
and anniversaries for readers to use!

Informative and entertaining—with notable
dates and trivia highlighted throughout the year.

Handy, convenient, pocketbook size to help you
keep track of your own personal important dates.

Added bonus—contains $5.00 worth of coupons
for upcoming Harlequin and Silhouette books.
This calendar more than pays for itself!

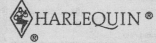

Available beginning in November at
your favorite retail outlet.

HARLEQUIN®   ***Silhouette®***

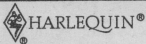

HARLEQUIN®

Don't miss these Harlequin favorites by some of our most distinguished authors! And now you can receive a discount by ordering two or more titles!

HT#25657	PASSION AND SCANDAL by Candace Schuler	$3.25 U.S. ☐ $3.75 CAN. ☐
HP#11787	TO HAVE AND TO HOLD by Sally Wentworth	$3.25 U.S. ☐ $3.75 CAN. ☐
HR#03385	THE SISTER SECRET by Jessica Steele	$2.99 U.S. ☐ $3.50 CAN ☐
HS#70634	CRY UNCLE by Judith Arnold	$3.75 U.S. ☐ $4.25 CAN. ☐
HI#22346	THE DESPERADO by Patricia Rosemoor	$3.50 U.S. ☐ $3.99 CAN ☐
HAR#16610	MERRY CHRISTMAS, MOMMY by Muriel Jensen	$3.50 U.S. ☐ $3.99 CAN. ☐
HH#28895	THE WELSHMAN'S WAY by Margaret Moore	$4.50 U.S. ☐ $4.99 CAN. ☐

(limited quantities available on certain titles)

AMOUNT	$
DEDUCT: 10% DISCOUNT FOR 2+ BOOKS	$
POSTAGE & HANDLING	$
($1.00 for one book, 50¢ for each additional)	
APPLICABLE TAXES*	$_____
TOTAL PAYABLE	$_____

(check or money order—please do not send cash)

To order, complete this form and send it, along with a check or money order for the total above, payable to Harlequin Books, to: **In the U.S.:** 3010 Walden Avenue, P.O. Box 9047, Buffalo, NY 14269-9047; **In Canada:** P.O. Box 613, Fort Erie, Ontario, L2A 5X3.

Name: _____

Address: _____ City: _____

State/Prov.: _____ Zip/Postal Code: _____

*New York residents remit applicable sales taxes.
 Canadian residents remit applicable GST and provincial taxes.   HBACK-OD3

Look us up on-line at: http://www.romance.net